# MAYBE MERMAIDS
# & ROBOTS ARE LONELY

*34 Stories and a Novella*

///////////////

## MATTHEW FOGARTY

**stillhouse
press**

Stillhouse Press is a student-run, non-profit literary organization.
All rights reserved.

**Stillhouse Press**
4400 University Drive, 3E4
Fairfax, VA 22030
www.stillhousepress.org

This is a work of fiction. Names, characters, places and incidents are
the product of the author's imagination. Any resemblance to actual
persons, living or dead, events or locales is entirely coincidental.

Matthew Fogarty's short stories have been widely published.
We would like to thank all of the places where his work first appeared,
including *alice blue review, Atticus Review, Belleville Park Pages,
Cosmonaut's Avenue, Day One, Everyday Genius, FRiGG Magazine, jmww,
Juked, Moon City Review, NANO Fiction, New Flash Fiction Review,
New South, PANK, Paper Nautilus, Passages North, Pinball, Pithead Chapel,
Vestal Review, Quiddity, Revolution John, A Sense of the Midlands Anthology*
(Muddy Ford Press, 2014), *Smokelong Quarterly, Squalorly, Story|Houston,
Sundog Lit,* and *Zero Ducats.*

**Library of Congress Control Number: 2016933443
ISBN-10: 0-9905169-4-1
ISBN-13: 978-0-9905169-4-1**

Printed in the United States of America

*Editor: Justin Lafreniere
Cover Design: Alex Walsh
Interior Design: Kady Dennell*

*This publisher is a proud member of*

# ADVANCE PRAISE FOR MATTHEW FOGARTY'S
## *MAYBE MERMAIDS & ROBOTS ARE LONELY*

"*Maybe Mermaids & Robots are Lonely* is a triumph of imagination, heart, and understated emotion. Each story transports the reader to a new dimension where the past and future mingle, where love and grief and loneliness are cast in intriguing new light. These are tales you'd trade on the playground in an alternate universe—a universe you won't want to leave after reaching the last page"

**KELLY LUCE, AUTHOR OF *THREE SCENARIOS IN WHICH HANA SASAKI GROWS A TAIL* AND *PULL ME UNDER***

"Along with the pure joy I felt while reading Matthew Fogarty's collection, I was reminded of something crucial: every storyteller is, at heart, lonely. It's why they tell their tales, because of this need to share, the need for the audience, the connection found in knowing. Whether it's a mermaid, a robot, or a zombie, Bigfoot, Andre the Giant, or the dinosaurs, Fogarty finds the inherent loneliness in all his heroes, the stark human desire to be a part of something larger than ourselves. Fogarty can be funny, ironic, clever, sad, or absurd, but no matter what hat he puts on, he has announced he is here, that he has joined the fray."

**MICHAEL CZYZNIEJEWSKI, AUTHOR OF *I WILL LOVE YOU FOR THE REST OF MY LIFE: BREAKUP STORIES***

"A marvelous collection, poignant and odd, whimsical and weighty. Matt Fogarty is a master of the short story form, giving weight and humanity to his characters even in the briefest of tales."

**TARA LASKOWSKI, AUTHOR OF *BYSTANDERS***

"Staggering in both its imaginative vision and in its remarkable sense of compression, Matthew Fogarty's work is like a narrative version of Joseph Cornell's window boxes: beautiful, surprising, remarkable, and endlessly entertaining. There's a golden thread here that connects Fogarty's vision to the likes of ETA Hoffmann and Richard Matheson, while, at the same, evoking the weird wit of Donald Antrim and George Saunders. But in the end, Fogarty's writing is mostly like itself: fun, weird, lovely, beautiful, and heartbreaking."

**CHRISTIAN KIEFER, AUTHOR OF _THE ANIMALS_**

"In this jewel box of a collection, Fogarty renders the fantastical as real, the real as fantastical. Millhauser-like, he gives human breath to even his most mythical of figures, convincing readers that the imaginary beings of our dreams actually live among us, swim, drive cars, have their hearts broken."

**DAVID BAJO, AUTHOR OF _MERCY 6_**

# CONTENTS

# UNDER

## MAYBE MERMAIDS & ROBOTS ARE LONELY

1

And just because his skin is steel doesn't mean he feels nothing. Maybe they're at a beach and she's in with the tide. Or maybe they're at the tops of skyscrapers, a city between them, and all they can see is each other: her with the curls that fall in a tangle over her shoulders and the dress that drapes her fins, him with the earnestness of a logic board. Wherever it is they find each other, he has to believe in the possibility, because if this isn't possible, what is?

Maybe they have coffee or a drink. She's intelligent, passionate about the sea. He's funny. She touches his arm and there's a spark. Later, they're at his factory, afterhours. In the breakroom, he finds salt and a jug of water. They lay under his favorite socket. He's barrel-chested, cylinder limbs heated drunk with her coursing energy. She's an electrical drug; her lips tap his circuit veins. He says, "I'd rust for you." She says, "You leave me breathless." Her grip is firm. His alloys green her clamshell breasts.

2

Maybe it's morning then and they're still at the factory when the first shift comes in.

Or maybe they woke early. They're already at the shore among schools of surfers. There's sand in his hinges; he feels unplugged. She says she has to go back. She says, "I wish you would come."

And maybe that's it. He lets her leave. Maybe his heart is a heat sink, a dull organ that shields his mainframe from her glow.

Or maybe it's clockwork, his heart, and maybe there's a screw that's twisted, a gear that slows. His LED eyes fade. There's an electric tear. He says, "I wish I could go."

A wave flows in. She ebbs out with it.

## 3

At the factory, he ratchets parts on the line, his hard drive looping that last image—her arms extended, hair trailing behind, the flip of a fin as she dives under, her wake shimmying the surface. Maybe that's when his memory loads an image of a surfer shedding a wetsuit.

In the closet, there are sheets of silicone rubber, bottles of glue and sealant, spools of thread. He lays them over a worktable, looms it all into the shape of him, his metal hands mechanical, methodical. If he could sweat, he'd wipe his brow. The moon sets in the high factory window.

## 4

At the beach, his pincers clamp at the sleeves, fit the wetsuit over his tin-can body. He goes awkwardly into the water, his feet softly sinking into the wet sand and the wet sand sucking thick against his step, against the pull and fall of his metal limbs. The water rises to his articulated joints and rises further. A broken wave washes against his mechanical chest, splashes the gloved whole of him, and recedes to the warm of the air. It splashes again, higher, and recedes again, the cool of it fogging the plastic mask he's sewn in to see. He loses his axis. The sea bottom descends. The sea floor gives way to water. He's surrounded by it. He's in it. His metal body buoys, and for a moment he floats, free—feels the surface as archived memory—before realizing it's a feeling he was never meant to have felt. He flails for it and from his flailing he floats down and he flails more and he goes deeper, floats further underwater, airless, deep and dumb.

He wonders whether robots can drown. He wonders whether she's forgotten him, or whether maybe he's in the wrong ocean, or if it's all just a cruel glitch. She's a failure of programming; she doesn't exist. Maybe this is what happens in the night, when the factory is closed and it's dark—idle robots dream of love and mermaids.

Or maybe that's when she catches him, thrashing for life, fishhooks her arms under his. He says, "I'm sorry. I'm not programmed to swim." And she smiles, takes his hand, says, "Then don't let go."

## RIVER TO SHANGHAI

Then, we lived next to a river and my brother spent a summer building a raft out of a fallen pine he claimed would float him down the river and out into the ocean and all the way to Shanghai. "May take a while," he'd say, "but I'll get there eventually." He told me all the things he expected to see on the way—tropical islands and whales and pirates and giant sea kelp and monsters—and described Shanghai as though it were paradise.

In our room one night, after we were supposed to have gone to sleep, he told me about some of the dreams he'd had, his adventures living there, this exotic land, having a whole house to himself. He said, "A young person like me can really make it in Shanghai. I can have any kind of family I want." This was the way he talked, like he was older than he really was and like there was a life that he wanted to live that was different from his own. He dreamed of being carried away from our real life, of new people and places. Even though I was younger than him, I understood what he meant. This was all during the time our parents were divorcing, when it seemed like home wasn't ours anymore.

When one day that fall he disappeared on his way home from school, I figured he'd done it—barged off down the grassy slope onto his pine raft, out into the open sea. Maybe he thought it would fix things, like he was the axe felling our family and that the family could only survive without him.

And for a time it was magic. Our parents were worried and the worrying together gave them something to talk about without fighting.

Each night they drove through the neighborhood together, called all the shelters and hospitals, talked to all his friends. I told them about the raft and the trip around the world. They hugged me and said I was sweet but that the story wasn't possible. Our backyard river was just a creek, they said, and beautiful as it is, it wouldn't have gotten him very far. Later that night they took me with them to search, Mom and me in the car, Dad in his waders kicking at the creek bottom.

Eventually, they each started to blame the other and they both blamed him. I started to miss him more than I was amazed by him. What he'd called adventure seemed more like escape—or even worse. And it wasn't long before we were back where we started. Except, across the dinner table now, instead of my living breathing brother, there was just a chair made of blonde wood and carved slats and blank space that seemed to bend light from the kitchen and collapse us toward it, our shoulders and our arms leaned toward nothing.

# PLAIN BURIAL

Bentley died somewhere in the middle of Nebraska. He was in the backseat and I didn't see him right away. I'd been giving him tranquilizers to help keep him calm on the trip out west, and when he laid down, I figured it was just the tranqs working too well. He wobbled a bit, looked woozy, and he did that low growl he does—more of a soft moan—when he wants something and doesn't know how to ask and I told him to shut up and I turned up the radio.

We'd been on the road since early in the morning when I snuck him out of the Holiday Inn. They had a no-pets policy and we skipped the free breakfast because of it. There wasn't any way we would've gotten out without them seeing him and so I took us both out the back door near where all the semis park. He dug a couple of holes and sniffed around and then stopped and got up on his haunches to shit and I said, "We gotta go, B," and yanked him out of it. I pulled over to the shoulder a few miles up and clipped on the leash and he ran around the ditch by the side of the highway for a couple minutes before finding his spot. He was always so regal, even in doing that; sometimes I'd offer him a newspaper to read. Still, I felt bad for the indignity of it, of having to do that basic living act with people speeding by. This time, he looked full of life, that big smile he'd get, like he was ready to run the rest of the way to San Francisco. And then some asshole in a Land Rover slowed and blew his horn and whooped at us. My awesome dog didn't hesitate: he barked and turned and shook his ass at the guy.

It wasn't until the truck stop outside of North Platte that I realized he'd stopped breathing. It was a Love's and there was a McDonald's inside and I lowered the windows a little and went in to get something to eat. I thought I'd seen his tail wag as I got out of the car. But he'd been quiet for much of the last hundred miles, and the longer I was in line, the more worried I got. I ordered him a breakfast sandwich and ran back to the parking lot. He was in the same position as when I left, his body stretched on its belly on the back seat, his head resting between his front paws, his eyes closed. I said his name a dozen times and leaned my head next to his, put my hand near his mouth and his nose. There was nothing.

It was not something I'd planned for. Yeah, he was getting old and he and I had been through a lot. I'd had him since he was two or three—those Lab eyes in the corner of the shelter were all I'd needed to see. Looking back on it, before we left Detroit, I had a feeling something bad might happen. It's like most days, you imagine yourself just existing where you are and, going someplace new, it's hard to see things working out perfectly, see all your life transplanted in one piece to a new place with new people. Everything feels uncertain. I was sure something would break. I just didn't think it'd be Bentley.

⁄⁄⁄⁄⁄⁄⁄⁄⁄⁄⁄⁄

The thing about having a dead dog in the car is that he starts to smell pretty much right away. All the gases and bodily fluids no longer serve a purpose and start to jailbreak. I grabbed an old sheet from a box in the trunk and tucked it under him, still hoping that at some moment his eyes would open and he'd get that long-mouthed smile and flip out his tongue at me and spray off a mohawk of slobber. It was his way of laughing. But he didn't move, his body weighed down, I suppose, by the lack of life.

Once I got the sheet all the way under him, I sat back down in the driver's seat and I lit up my phone and started Googling where we were and how far we were from San Francisco and what the hell to do. In those first minutes, there was just that drained feeling in the stomach, or maybe it's a draining feeling. Something about to escape either way. And I looked up into the rearview and saw him shrouded on the backseat and that's when I burst. It's just that we'd spent so many nights, just me and him. He'd make faces and fold his body in all kinds of ways, bury his head in my armpit or my lap or lay across my feet or follow me when I got up for whatever reason and then beat me back to the sofa, leaping into my seat before I got there, and he'd do his mohawk laugh. I'd ventroliquize, give him words. Make him sound like a better version of me. Happier.

Ashley'd just woken up when I called. "It's beautiful out," she said. "The fog burned off early. We should be eating pancakes."

"Yeah, that sounds great," I said. I imagined her in a pink tee shirt and underwear, hair in a ponytail, in the bed we bought together last time I visited. "Hey something happened." She asked what it was and I told her about Bentley. Tried to, anyway. I said, "I got—there's this breakfast sandwich. It's on the seat next to me. Bentley's—"

"What is it?"

"He's—" My mind filtered through all the kinder ways to describe it: passed, lost, kicked the bucket, no longer with us, and so on. But all that came out was, "Fuck. He's gone. Bentley's dead."

"Oh, I'm sorry. Babe, that sucks," she said.

"Yeah."

"I know how much you loved him." There was something in me that thought it didn't sound right, the way she said it. And it occurred to me then that she'd only met him the one time—last Christmas when she flew to Detroit and I showed her around the suburbs I grew up in and we went over to my parents' house for dinner. My dad loved her and my mom did too, once she was able to look past the fact there was some woman other than her in my life now. She'd always warned me against committing to someone too quickly, before seeing what kind of friend they'd make, but I told her Ashley and I'd had some great times together, that we were in love, and she seemed to agree that this was enough. Bentley was unsure even after Ashley gave him a treat and took him for a walk. Those nights, he'd climb onto the bed and lie down between us, force us to move to the edges. I proposed anyway, and we spent that New Year's outside along the riverwalk in the cold, watching the fireworks reflect on the ice. It wasn't ever a question for me, but still we had a long talk on Skype about whether or not I should bring him.

"Is there a morgue or something you can take him to?"

"I don't know." I can't leave him here, I thought. "It's Sunday in Nebraska. I think everything's probably closed."

"I can search the Internet for you if you need."

"It's okay. I've got my phone."

"What would you even do with a dead dog? Maybe, like, a pet cemetery? Do those really exist?"

"Probably. I don't know. We only have twenty hours from here. I can't think right now."

"We used to flush our goldfish down the toilet."

"He's not a goldfish."

"I know."

"I can't leave him here."

"Is there a hardware store that's open?"

"Probably. Why?"

"Just—you could find a spot in a forest, maybe? Somewhere he'd be peaceful?"

"Bury him? I'm—I'm in Nebraska."

"I don't know. I'm sorry. I'm trying to help. There's got to be somewhere."

"Seriously, I can't leave him here."

"Okay, but you're not going to drive twenty hours with a dead dog in the car. That's ridiculous."

I said I didn't know and told her I'd call her later.

"I love you," she said.

"Yeah."

I looked again to the backseat, just to see if Bentley had moved, if maybe he was joking or begging for attention. He would do that sometimes and the longer we were together the more I found myself mimicking him with Ashley. Like the morning after she and I first slept together and I pretended to have a heart attack and pass out and she smiled and laughed and slapped my stomach. More than anything, I remember the light in her bedroom that morning, the sun filtering through her sheer curtains and the way it made everything seem so alive—her dark hair lit up blonde, the way she squinted with the light and without her glasses.

We'd met in line at a taco shop in Austin just as she was graduating law school and moving west and I was leaving grad school and moving home. There was that first intense spring month when we saw each other every night and there wasn't any pressure because we were both leaving and we let ourselves explore and risk things because of it. There was the way her naked body reacted when I curled up behind it, pressed back into mine feet first and then legs and then back like we were being zipped together, like the closing of a warm jacket. There were Skype calls and a bunch of trips to California after that, some more fun than others, some good days and great nights and a whole bunch of mornings too, but there was something so sunlit natural about that first one that made us desperate to reproduce it.

I'd left Bentley with my parents that year I was in Texas and I felt alone in the world because of it. Most times I didn't have any doubt about Ashley; there were so many things that just felt right or at least more right than they'd felt with the other women I'd dated since college. And when one of her friends at the Academy of Sciences was hiring for an assistant curator, I was convinced there was some kind of fate thing going on that was pushing us together. But then, if I'm being honest, there were a few times I questioned things, when I wondered whether she and I would have fallen in love so quickly if Bentley had been there with me.

///////////

North Platte didn't look like much more than a typical Oregon Trail stagecoach stop. Other than a couple of main streets in the center, it was mostly the big box stores and Walmarts and generic whatever stores that keep people trapped in these boring small towns. Even if he'd been alive, Bentley probably would've slept through it. And for that reason alone, it didn't seem right to leave him there. Even if I'd wanted to, according to the Humane Society's website, the necessary city services were mostly nonexistent on the weekends. Breaking into a pet cemetery afterhours felt like the start of a bad horror novel. And the shallow roadside grave option was also wrong. Unlike most dogs, he wasn't a big fan of the road. Without drugs, he'd get nauseous after a few miles, pace the backseat, and hang his face out the window, sick. It just wouldn't be peaceful.

I thought about the river, the Platte. He loved the water, loved chasing thrown rocks to the lake bottom, and I thought maybe I could build a little raft and send him off to wherever rivers go. There was that brief moment of fantasy—Bentley cast off into the sunset like a dead Huck Finn—until I realized the river probably runs through someone's backyard at some point and that there'd probably be some kid that'd have to go on living his life having once found Bentley's decomposed body tied to a crude raft of sticks.

More than anything, I wanted him to come with me, both so I could be with him and he could be with me. He'd saved my life so many times.

So I drove.

I didn't know where else to go and still didn't know what to do. At the edge of town, there was a hardware store called Ben's Hardware, and it looked open, so I pulled into the dirt parking lot thinking maybe I'd come up with something. It was an old wood building, detached and away from the rows of sad downtown storefronts. There were bells strung to the door, and inside, it smelled thick and sweet like old wood. The floors creaked. The old man behind the counter said hello and I didn't really feel like talking, so I just nodded and kept going like I already knew where to find what I wanted. I assumed he was Ben, though his workshirt nametag said "Bill."

The aisles were small and overcrowded and there were poles and fishing tackle hanging from the ceiling. In the back of the store, there was a section of camping supplies—compasses and knives and air mattresses and camp stoves and coolers, those kinds of things. "Need some help?" asked Ben or Bill, who had followed me.

And that's when the plan came together in my head: get a cooler, fill it with ice, and lift sheet-wrapped Bentley into it. "I need a big cooler," I said.

"How big?"

"Big enough for a black Lab."

Bill-Ben smiled, deepening the ruts at the corners of his eyes. "Ha!" He looked at me, maybe waiting for me to say something. It was a thing Bentley used to do whenever I'd come home. And with that thought I had to clench my lips and my eyes and I looked back toward the shelves.

"Oh shit," said Bill-Ben. "I'm sorry, friend."

"It's okay."

"I didn't realize. My boy Roscoe, he died a year ago." He had a hard time saying this. His hands looked weathered. "You're not from here."

"No. Traveling," I said. "I can't leave him."

"I know it. You can't. I'm sorry," he said. "Biggest we got is fifty quarts. You probably need something bigger. Probably need a marine cooler. What's his name?"

"Bentley."

"Sounds like a big boy."

"Yeah."

"You probably need the seventy-five. Young's Marine down by the river. Except he's not open today."

"There's nowhere else in town?"

"Don't think so. There're the big places, but not for this."

"No."

"I mean, the fifty might work. I just—if you buy it and it doesn't work, I'm not going to be able to refund that money."

"I know," I said. I bought the cooler, took it out to the parking lot, and set it on the ground near the back of the car.

"Need some help?" Bill-Ben asked, again having followed.

"That'd be great."

"Not something you plan for."

"It's really not," I said. I opened the car and the force of the smell pushed me backward. It was off-putting. There was the familiar sweaty smell of Bentley somewhere in it, but it was overtaken by the rest—mothball death and must and bitter and shit.

"How long's he been gone?" asked Bill-Ben.

"Just a couple hours. We're headed to San Francisco."

"Wow. That's a thing."

"My girlfriend suggested I"—I started to say dump—"bury him by the side of the road."

"No. You can't do that." He stepped in front of me, moved the cooler to the ground below the backseat, opened it, and lifted the two ends of the sheet to test Bentley's weight. "Beautiful boy," he said.

I said yeah and he pointed me toward the other side of the car. "Get in there and hold his head. I'll pull him out. Might fit after all."

We moved him gently, like a wounded soldier, lifting the four corners of the sheet slowly and keeping him from hitting the roof of the car. When he was halfway out and Bill-Ben had started positioning the bottom of him in the cooler, I walked back around to help.

With his legs and tail folded under and his back arched and his nose straight ahead, he just barely fit in the open cooler. I had to press the top of his head down, point his nose at the ground, to be able to close the lid. He looked ashamed, like he'd gotten into something he shouldn't have. I imagined him saying sorry: *Sorry for having ruined the drive, sorry for stinking up the car, sorry for every time I made you feel like I wasn't listening, sorry for not being there in Austin.* I guessed then that *sorry* was better than *I told you so.*

"Convenience store up the way," Bill-Ben said after we got the cooler up onto the backseat. "Get some ice, right? Cover him over. You can get back on the highway from there, make it straight through to wherever."

"Thanks," I said and shook his hand. I didn't know what else to say. I was still thinking about what to do with my buddy, where to let him rest for good. Bill-Ben stood there too in the sun, both of us probably thinking the same thought—something about what it means to be a friend and how rare a thing it is to find a good one.

"Well, good luck to you."

"Thanks," I said. "Hey, I'm Sam."

"Roger," he said. He saw me look at the nametag and smiled. "Yeah, wife got it at a Goodwill. Nice and soft and worn in."

"I love old shirts too," I said. "I really appreciate the help."

"Anytime," he said and walked back to the store.

///////////

What you have to understand about Bentley is that he was a dreamer. Most nights he'd take up half the bed, sprawled out on his side, paws toward my chest, and I'd wake up in the middle of the night to the paws twitching and his closed eyes twitching and his mouth twitching. His legs would flex and I could see him running and leaping in his dream. I always wondered what he dreamed about, where he was. And maybe it's selfish or vain to think, or maybe it's just the personality I've made up for him, but I liked to think that maybe every once in a while he dreamed about saving me from something. I had saved him plenty of times from cars or other dogs or chocolate, and I figured it was what we did. Part of our deal. We looked out for each other in our own ways. Sometimes

I'd come home and he would be up on the windowsill watching for me, watching to make sure I got in safely. Or maybe he dreamed about Saturdays, chasing Frisbees, the racetrack path he'd wear around the living room for no reason, just because, clearing the couch in two bounds, his paws barely touching it.

It had taken fifteen hours to get to North Platte what with us stopping every hundred miles or so for food or a walk, and I made it back to my parents' house an hour quicker. I called Ashley when we were halfway home, told her I'd be a few days later than we planned. She said she wasn't upset, just that she didn't get it. I told her I didn't expect she would and that I needed some time to think about things. As much as I wanted to picture her crying, pulling off the ring I'd given her, making sad margaritas with her friends, I could only imagine her going through her day like nothing happened. Maybe she'd even be a little happy as she returned the special vacuum she'd bought to clean up the dog hair.

The light at the bottom of the exit ramp was red and something hit me then: that it was where, if we'd been on a long trip, Bentley would realize we were almost home and he'd stand up and press his face against my ear, like he was driving too. He'd do that all the way to my parents' house.

Their cars weren't in the driveway so I parked and got out and entered the code to raise the garage door. It was getting colder out with the sun going down earlier and the red-oranging trees that always made me feel like those afternoons I'd come home from school and there wouldn't be anyone in the house and it'd just be my parents' dog and me or then later Bentley and me. I took my dad's shovel, the one he uses on the driveway after a snow, and put it in the trunk on top of all my things and drove back through the subdivision.

I took us to the park—his favorite park—with the merry-go-round I'd once convinced him to jump and spin on. He thought it was hilarious and he did his round laugh and he tried to tackle me but he was too dizzy to see and ended up in the dirt under a bush, which was the only decent place I could think worthy of saying goodbye, of leaving him for good. And so I grabbed the shovel and rolled the cooler out onto the grass to the middle of the park to the bush and started to dig deep into the dirt, deep until I found just the right spot.

# BEACH GLASS

You were in the kitchen and there was fog outside. We could hear the wind even over the running water, the wind whipping the branches of trees, one branch thrashing out of the milk-white, slapping at the window, and disappearing again. The glass you were holding slipped and broke. It was the glass we bought that summer in France, near the ocean. The tall glass with seashells on it. We bought it at that roadside stand we'd biked to after leaving our hotel, where earlier we'd decided it was time. We were ready. We made the little one. We knew it even then, the way you slid your hips under mine, tilted.

We kept the glass as a souvenir. It reminded us both of the morning and of the teenager who ran the roadside stand with her mother—the girl's flowing skirt, her sand-streaked hair, leaning back into her mother. The smile of her mother. What we wanted our girl to be.

Later, there was the gray wrinkled man we met on the train who spent the whole trip through the Alps talking about his own daughter, about how she'd grown up slower than others say, how even then she needed him, how he had to believe she needed him. He talked slowly. He took long pauses between thoughts. You held your headphones at your neck, kept waiting for him to finish, until in one mountain pass, he said something about your hands, how soft they looked, how much they reminded him of his daughter's hands and his own hands as a child. Like we're all trees in the same forest, he said.

And then with our daughter, who'd struck where you were sore and run out and who, now, had come back for help. You with your hand bleeding. You turned back toward her, told her she'd gone wrong, shouldn't have run out in the first place, should've stayed in the house like we asked. Like she deserved it. That she would flirt with a stranger and get caught in a bad spot. She was bleeding too. You from the glass, she from the bad spot, the two of you standing in drip-fed estuaries of your own blood. You didn't see it, but they flowed together, lazy thin rivers that pooled in the middle of the kitchen tile, the pine-patterned linoleum we bought soon after she was born. I could hear the wind even over your crying. I had to take her out of there.

In the car, I told her you hadn't meant it. That you were sorry. That you loved her. And that's when she started bleeding more and I drove faster. It was hard to see in the fog with the wind and the branches coming out of nowhere. The whole world just car and branches and blood.

I called you from the hospital. You were still upset, still in tears, torn. And it cut into me then. That there wasn't anything left of us. That we'd fallen apart, you and me. Neither of us could speak. We just breathed there together with phones in our hands, our hands soft from the water and everything else.

## WE ARE SWIMMERS

Something got stirred up between us here at the bottom of this great lake. Like a minute ago the water was blue-green and we could see each other through it, see our blue-green faces and hazel eyes. But now there's dirt floating free up from the lakebed, a cloud of particulate mud, Loch Nessian, and we're down here straining for breath within it. Both of us rathering to drown in the mire than float to the surface and see again. Both of us rathering to grow gills, to grow fins, to mermaid and merman ourselves, to transform our human bodies and spend our stardust lives swimming this silty freshwater necklace of glacial lakes. We think that'll solve it, that neither of us'll see the other cry if our whole together world is wet. And so we look only forward, ignoring the four brackish streams tiding back past our estuary tails.

## CARDBOARD GRACELAND

Fat Elvis makes me sad. So after a few years playing the Boardwalk, when the rhinestones started popping off my peacock jumpsuit, I gave up the room at the Y near the beach and moved back into my parents' basement out in the suburbs. Like all basements, it's a dingy space with a gray cement floor, all sawdust and chalk from when my dad used to keep his tools down here. But I've got my own private entrance from the backyard and there's a toilet in one corner and I've done some things to really make the space my own. Laid down a few leopard-print rugs Elvis would've liked and tacked up some insulation so I can perform without the neighbors interrupting. Found a can of gold paint on sale and took it to a couple of the walls. Tacked up some of my old records and my velvet Elvis. Made it feel like home.

The biggest thing, though, the thing I'm most proud of, is this: a few months ago I was driving around looking for dumpster treasures to sell or keep, maybe. I was in my mom's pink Mary Kay Cadillac, the one she got back in the '70s for being one of their top sellers, the car she drove cross-country to see the King live in Vegas, the car she says I was conceived in with "Don't Be Cruel" on the eight-track. And in the parking lot of a strip mall, back behind a Home Depot, there was a pile of refrigerator cartons leaning against a dumpster—big cardboard shipping containers for the huge refrigerators people get now, with the icemakers and computers inside. Immediately I saw what they could be, and I loaded them into the trunk and took them home and through my door into the basement. I spent a week building them together with duct tape. Turned my basement into the interior of Graceland.

Obviously, I had to do it to scale, and it wasn't possible to make it three levels like the original. I had to choose which rooms were most important. When you come down the stairs, there's the Jungle Room with the rugs and the couch and to the left there's Elvis' bedroom. There's the kitchen where I make my sandwiches. I bought more gold paint and some other prints and brought in all my memorabilia and it all looks rich and beautiful, just like Elvis. And then, of course, I built a cardboard wall around the toilet and took some of my other dumpster finds and decorated the bathroom as well as I could. They don't let just anyone see the throne where the King died. All I had were secret pictures I found on the Internet.

The rooms are smaller than Elvis was used to and not as opulent and sometimes when it's dark I knock into the cardboard and spend the next morning patching walls. There're three doors between the TV room and the bedroom and my bed isn't as big as Elvis'. Makes it hard to sleep like him. And I haven't used the toilet. It just feels wrong. I go upstairs to my parents' bathroom, which is the only time I see real sun some days. Some days when I feel sick or extra sad I go to the bathroom door and touch the cardboard knob, the same way I think Elvis would have, gentle and unsure, and sometimes it helps, makes me feel better to think for a second that Elvis and I are going through the same kind of stuff.

I haven't had any of the crazy parties Elvis used to have. But once my Graceland was finished, I put on my song machine and my show clothes and sang the setlists from all the concerts, start to finish, the famous ones and the ones no one talks about. Some of those shows were pretty great. I even did the movies, acted out all the scenes, sang the lines. And then yesterday I got to the Pittsburgh show, New Year's Eve 1977, and I kept going until late, sang "It's Now or Never" at midnight like he would've wanted. Only slept for that month-long break before the last tour.

There're so many things about our lives that are the same. That first summer on the Boardwalk, I was the star attraction. One afternoon I played to a whole tour bus. Three hour set. Aced the whole catalog. I said I was done and they went wild for more. One lady tossed me her panties. That gig was my *Ed Sullivan* moment.

I always admired how much Elvis loved to be on stage, how he loved to make other people happy, invite them into his world for a night. They had to pull him off the stage. That's why I went to the Boardwalk in the first place: to be entertaining and make other people smile. I felt like I was really doing something. Even when my own life was shit hard— couldn't ever keep a job, couldn't keep up with classes in school, drugs, couldn't stay straight, always something going wrong, the loneliness— the idea I could do what Elvis did made it all worth it. I like to think he and I figured it out at the same point in our lives, that one man working for himself isn't anything, but one man working for everybody else is something. He didn't know Pittsburgh would be one of his last concerts. But I knew it. I couldn't un-know it. And it made me sad to think the end of things was soon.

I thought I'd do something special, thought I'd sing Elvis' last shows for everybody at the beach, my own last show. I figured if things went well I could make it a bigger thing, do a whole series of shows, like Elvis' last tour. Make some posters, maybe.

So this afternoon I trimmed my burns and pulled on the jumpsuit and I went to the Boardwalk. It'd been raining. The air was hot and humid and I was sweating and the wet shorted one of my amps, cut out halfway through my entrance music. I tried to do my big karate kick, but the seams on my suit split under the arms and I had to stop. There weren't many people out except for some teenagers, surf kids probably, and they stopped whatever they were doing to watch and laugh. I've got a wireless mic that lets me roam a bit and work the crowd, and since they were my only crowd I tried to banter. Asked where they were from. They laughed and one of them called me a fat old loser and another one called me the worst Elvis he'd ever seen. Tall blonde kid with a backwards baseball cap said I was a "faggot with bitch tits."

I could sense it then, that there was a turn in things. And it was the turn that made me understand Elvis even more, made me understand why he took drugs, why he wanted to "Make the World Go Away." I couldn't help it, I got distracted. Missing cues, losing lyrics. Just like Elvis' last special, the thing he did for CBS, when halfway into "Are You Lonesome Tonight" he lost his place and started cracking jokes. Except I couldn't think of anything good. I guess Elvis was a little quicker in the head than me. I said something like, "My mom says my 'Hound Dog' is better than Elvis' 'Hound Dog,'" which she really did say once, but it didn't help. The kids just stood there laughing and calling me names and taking pictures with their cellphones.

I thought about what Elvis would do. Those last shows when he started to lose it, when the crowd began to yell, he'd stop it short. Figured it was better to give them a couple of good songs than to work through a painful set. I hadn't made any money and I knew whatever I did these teenagers weren't going to give it up. And there was some great loneliness that had filled me so full I could barely see. So I shut the music off and went home.

At the house, there was that razor smell of fresh-cut grass that sticks up in your nose and cuts into it. Inside, the basement smelled like Elvis, like Graceland, except it was my smell too, like I'd made it my own.

That's all how I got to where I am now, at the door to the bathroom, just like Elvis, and to the sink and to the toilet and to the bathroom floor next to the toilet, just like Elvis. Try to stand but it's blurry, just like Elvis. Fall sideways into the cardboard walls, through the walls of my Graceland, through the cardboard and the duct tape. And I bring them all down. Just like Elvis.

## PEARLS

I saw a kid slice through his hand one night at the Oyster Bar and it kind of set a bad tone. I was on a date with a woman I'd met online. Her profile said she was adventurous and liked seafood, and I'm adventurous and like seafood, and so I sent her a message even though we were only a fifty-nine percent match. I decided to be a little more forward than usual: *Do you believe in soulmates?* I asked. *Based on your profile, I believe you could be mine.*

She replied within an hour: *Sure, what the hell. Let's get oysters.*

Oysters. The ultimate aphrodisiac. We ordered two dozen.

I was in my seersucker; she was in a bright orange dress. Her laugh was more like a crow's *caw* than anything human. Her lipstick was crooked and her teeth were too white. She smelled of the sea. But I was sure she had a good heart.

And there, too, was the college kid on the other side of the metal bar. He brought out a bucketful from the back, threw a white towel over his shoulder, and started jabbing his knife into the shells and pounding them on a wood block. I could tell he was new: his hands were shaky and his grip kept slipping—first the oyster shell, then the knife handle too. Nor did he throw out any witty banter like the other shuckers.

Not that we paid much attention. We were engaged in that typical first date tête-à-tête. She used all her body to flirt, especially her legs, and the conversation was thick and layered. We disagreed about the meanings of things—religious signs and sacrifices, foreign aid, the confederate flag. Part of me wanted to fast-forward to an anniversary, years from now, when we'd look back on this awkward time as the start of our complex and dynamic relationship. I was tired of dating, tired of eating alone. Supermarkets don't sell bachelor portions.

And that's when it happened. I turned toward the kid just as the shell slipped and the knife caromed off it and into the flesh of the kid's palm. He let out a coarse shriek. It was the first time I'd seen a tendon, though I didn't get a great look before the whole hand spilled over with blood.

The other guys were Johnnies-on-the-spot with it, and they had towels out even before most of the other people at the bar fully realized what had happened.

They got the kid off to the hospital and the manager, who had a starfish splatter of blood on his shirt, was apologetic. But we were both a little traumatized and I'd lost my appetite so we decided to end the date there. As we got up to leave, I noticed a smear of something red below her lip—blood, maybe, or cocktail sauce. Before I could offer her a napkin, she turned away toward the manager and asked sweetly if she could have a bag of discarded shells to take home. I thought for a moment there was hope; I formed this romantic image in my mind of her making some sort of macramé art or creating an oyster garden off of which the sun would glint at just the right angle, cast a ray through her kitchen window, light her from just the right angle to highlight her true goodness inside. Without hesitating, he loaded a bucket's worth into a couple of takeout bags, which she hoisted over her shoulder along with her purse.

Outside on the sidewalk, we paused under a streetlamp in that typical, goodnight-is-goodbye way that all my dates, full-length or aborted, seemed to end, like there in the cold we were searching each other for any last piece of either of us the other might care to be curious about. She saw my eyes settle on the bag.

"Fertilizer," she said. "They make great fertilizer. Although really if I'm being honest, I just like them for the smell—the smell of old seafood." And with that she laughed and walked off into the night.

## FROZEN ALIVE

No way those are legs, I said, but Chris was already halfway across the room and I skated after him to the empty elevator shaft to check. We had sneaked under the fence of the abandoned auto plant down near the highway overpass after some of the kids at school heard from someone that a water pipe had burst in there and the floor froze over. Chris said it'd probably be good ice, too, especially when our regular pond was getting pounded by sleet that seemed like it might never stop. So we both grabbed our sticks and called around to the other guys and we all went down there.

We found a low hole in the fence and crawled on our stomachs and then there was a long blank space of white untouched snow. At that point I was thinking the story would turn out to be bullshit. I didn't see any tracks from anybody or anything else being there and the whole area looked like it'd been bombed out, with the crumbling walls and the exposed steel and the loose wires like you see in war movies. But sure enough, once we got in, there it was: a whole factory floor covered over solid with thick ice so clean, in the right light, you could see through it. We had to have been the first ones to even think of playing in there. And our voices made this creepy echo that just kept going.

We set up the nets and picked teams and then halfway into the first period, I wound up for a slap shot and drove it off the post into another room that must've been a lobby or something back when they used the place. Chris and I went to go find the puck, skating in through the doorway, grabbing hold of the sides to keep our balance on the fresh ice.

It was dark in there but we could see what used to be the building entrance, probably long before the outside windows and doors got boarded up and across from it there were a bunch of elevator shafts. Whatever burst must have been a pretty big pipe (it would've been cool to watch) because those shafts were all full up with ice too. And right there were the two somethings sticking up out of one of them.

Chris was like, there's a dead guy in there. And at first I didn't believe him. The place looked deserted, for one, and just the way the guy would have had to be positioned it seemed crazy that somebody would fall into the shaft and the water would freeze at exactly that moment. Besides, Chris had been talking a lot about seeing dead guys since his brother went off to Afghanistan. In fact, he'd been giving me some shit about it too, like my brother was a wuss because he wouldn't sign up and he was going to stick around and try to play pro hockey instead. Chris kept saying he wasn't good enough, that my brother was just afraid. And he was probably right: we all knew he'd end up a mechanic or unemployed or something.

Anyway, I just wanted to grab the puck and get out but Chris wouldn't let it go and he skated over to the elevator shaft where it was real dark. I didn't want him to think I was scared so I went over too, and yeah, turned out they were legs. Two thick legs cut off by the ice at the knees, with fallen brown suitpants and brown socks and shoes. They were in a sort of v-shape, like they were flailing when they froze, like the guy didn't mean to fall in or he did mean to and he just had this one second of regret on the way in but it was too late.

Probably homeless, Chris said. Pretty fucking sad way to die.

Chris is a big kid and it's always weird to see big kids cry. There he got really small like with his shoulders in and his head down and he started doing this spasm thing, just pitching forward a few times. He wouldn't look at me. He acted like it was nothing. He bent down and tried to see further under the ice, but there wasn't much else he could see, and he stood up again when we heard the others skating in toward us. Everybody thought it was kind of cool and spooky and they took turns looking in the shaft but I don't think anybody saw much else either. Certainly no one could see his face all the way down there. Although, I kind of saw it, I think, or maybe it was just that I had pictured him pretty strongly in my mind.

We called the game after that and all went home and didn't tell anybody what we'd seen. Nobody wanted to get in trouble for breaking in there, and we all figured too that if somebody cared about him they'd have kept him from diving into the shaft in the first place. Chris never mentioned it again, not even when it was just the two of us, though I imagine he probably told his brother once he got back from overseas. They talk about everything.

But I watched him all that night and most nights after, falling over and over while I was trying to sleep. And now that it's summer and the ice is gone I've been wondering more what happened to the body. I wonder whether they found it once we left and chiseled him out with an ice axe. Or whether he's still there in the melt, his body wet, afloat in a puddle at the bottom of the shaft. Or whether when the ice thawed maybe he thawed too, whether his blood warmed to normal and he came back to life and his eyes opened and he just sprang up and stretched and went on his way.

# OVER

## BIGFOOT'S OVERCOAT

We figured if there's anyone you could trust with a secret it'd be Bigfoot. He sat in the records room in a corner of the back hall past the copier and we barely ever saw him. He was just one of those guys, five thirty and he's out the door, nothing left but footprints. Maybe every once in a while, as the elevator doors closed, you'd catch the tail of that ratty old overcoat he wore, but he'd never come to happy hour with the rest of the office and he wasn't a big talker. I'm not sure we ever heard him say more than the occasional "hello" or "leave it there" or "Mondays, right?" Mostly, he'd just grumble or roar. And that's why Lisa and I thought we could trust him.

It was just one of those things, her and me. No one else knew about the two of us, and since we got together, we'd worked hard to keep it that way. I joined Nicholson straight out of law school. Lisa started a year later and they put her on the back hall with me and all the other junior associates. We were all working on the same reinsurance settlement, the team billing who knows how many hours, late nights and weekends in the office, while the partners were doing their thing keeping the client satisfied and paying. So she and I would have a drink after work some nights, or sometimes during our short break before heading back to the office.

But until the happy hour two months ago there wasn't anything more to it. We both stayed later than usual, had a couple more than we meant to, and decided to share a taxi home. We went to her house first, and as she leaned in to hug me goodbye, she turned her head and slid her lips across mine—almost as if by accident—but then a second later her lips came back and we kissed. One of those magic-electric kisses that feels like licking a lightbulb in a hot shower. An all-of-a-sudden thing. We went inside and spent the night like that, the two of us on her couch, kissing. We stopped short of sex. We knew we needed to be careful.

It's not technically against the rules for two associates to date, but no one who has still works here. Nicholson considers it disruptive and disloyal. And because not many of the associates here love their lives, they tend to get envious if they see others sharing any form of happiness. In a law firm, envy's a dangerous thing: it turns people into monsters, shifts them from jealous to hostile to political to warlike. Maybe somebody gets upset about something work-related and gets the idea to take one or both of us down. All they'd have to do is mention our relationship to one of the partners, and suddenly we're getting bad looks, bad assignments, bad bonuses. Soon enough, we're looking for new jobs.

Plus, there was something so unexpectedly exciting about being together that we wanted to explore it without everybody watching. So, we kept it quiet, and for two months, we'd been going strong.

Except it really weighs on you, keeping a secret like that. You can't touch. Can't look each other in the eyes. Can't buy each other lunch or drinks. You have to see around corners, meet on other sides of the city, kiss in dark alleys. You have to ask the stupid Monday morning questions, like "How was your weekend?", even when you spent the whole weekend together. You have to have cover stories, cover identities, disguises. The longer we stayed stealth, the more we both needed someone to talk to.

///////////

Bigfoot started on a Tuesday a month or so ago. Nicholson hired him through a temp agency to fill in for Cheryl, our pregnant records clerk. Her water had burst earlier than planned, and she was gone that Monday, so with no one around to train him, they just sort of locked him up in the records room without any real orientation.

I stopped by on his first day to make him feel welcome. Cheryl collects Pez and he was moving them one by one into a desk drawer. He was about seven feet tall, a hairy stuffed animal, like you'd want to hug him and he'd keep you safe at night. Except his claws were long and he smelled rancid, like a dog that had peed itself and hadn't ever been dried off. I stood in the doorway and said, "Hi," and "I'm Pete," and "Let me know if there's anything you need." And he turned and showed me his teeth, said an angry "Hello" and grunted like he was annoyed or bothered, so I kept walking.

We've had a lot of temps come through our office. They're cheaper for Nicholson since the firm doesn't have to pay benefits and they can fire them anytime they want without anyone really caring. In my experience, temps come in two breeds: crazy and shy. And while they're all decent at most things, none of them are particularly great at anything.

Bigfoot was one of the shy ones. Most days he'd stay locked up in the records room, wearing his overcoat and that red '70s skinny tie he always wore, alone behind the desk with Cheryl's ergonomic keyboard and a stinky forest of old files. He'd always go in and out the back door, straight to the elevators. He could've taken two-hour lunches and none of us would've known. You might've thought he was in trouble with the law or running from something, that temping was a way of hiding in plain sight, staying out of a trap.

We found if you brought him a cruller and sat with him in his office, and if you could stand the smell, he'd take the bait and listen. And Bigfoot was a great listener. Real compassionate and soft. Tender eyes. All the associates went to him with secrets. Lisa was the first. She walked in there one Thursday morning out of desperation or habit, maybe; she and Cheryl used to talk all the time.

I was in the copy room at the time and I tried to hear her through the wall, but it was too thick and all I could pick up were soft vibrations, incomprehensible mumbles. Bigfoot's response to everything was somewhere between a grunt and a howl and I couldn't tell whether that was good or bad. Whatever it was, I saw her go in there the next day, too. And then later that week when I knew Lisa was in the copy room, I stepped into Records just to show her I wasn't afraid.

It was like a cage in there—rows of filing cabinets, stacks and stacks of unsorted folders. Bigfoot was behind the desk sitting shorter than I expected. He ended up on a stool, probably because they couldn't find a chair he'd fit in. The lighting in the records room isn't great and he was hard to see. Without saying anything, I set a donut on the desk between us and he reached his paw across and took it. There was something in his eyes, some sweet depth to them, as he leaned forward in the sweaty stench of his office and started nibbling.

I hesitated a second and he waved me forward with his paw. With that, I just let loose: "She's the most beautiful woman I've ever slept with. It's more than that. It's an adventure. Like we're spies or something. And sure, there are things I don't love. But do you have to love everything about someone? Or is 'almost' enough?" He shrugged at this, did that moan/growl thing. He mumbled a "Sure, sure," and it was relieving in a way I can't describe. Validating. I'd felt all this pressure eating a hole through my stomach and, in truth, I realize now that I wasn't looking for advice anyway; it was good just to get it out, to talk to someone who seemed to understand.

Lisa mentioned to Robyn that she'd had a good session with Bigfoot and so, the next day, Robyn was in there talking about I don't know what. Abraham followed. His wife'd had a miscarriage and I'm sure it was probably bothering him, that maybe he felt guilty about something. He never seemed like he was ready to be a dad. And there were others I saw go in to talk things out. It just became the thing to do in the office. We'd all go talk to Bigfoot.

*////////////*

I've mentioned Bigfoot's overcoat. It was one of those tan floor-length coats you see in some of the nicer shops, except that on Bigfoot it only came down to his knees, leaving his furry calves exposed. It was a thin material—can't have been very warm—and it looked like it'd been beaten with rocks and dragged through mud. And the shoulders were a little too small and sometimes when he'd turn the stitches would pop.

Once, when I was in his office, I suggested he ought to replace it. "Maybe you could find something cheap at a Goodwill," I said.

He howled at this, like he was saying *No way*. Offended, I thought. Maybe at me assuming a temp couldn't afford a new coat. Maybe out of pride, like there was no way a used coat would be acceptable. Or maybe like this one had some kind of sentimental value, some heirloom passed down through generations of bigfoots. Whatever it was, he stood, his head almost hitting the low fluorescent light in that dark room, and he puffed out his chest and swiped at me with one of those huge paws. "I'm sorry," I said. "I didn't mean anything by it." This was right around the end of the day and he walked over to the coat rack and shoved his arms into the overcoat over his plaid polyester suit and he turned his head back toward me. He had this look like he'd really shown me something, like he'd proved something. It was the closest to smiling I'd ever seen him come.

///////////

The reinsurance settlement case finished up a little over a week ago and the whole office, partners included, went down to Harry's Giant Texas Tap Room for a massive happy hour celebration. I stopped by Bigfoot's office to see if maybe, this time, he'd come with us. He already had his overcoat on and was headed toward the elevators. "The partners are buying," I said. "It'll be fun. It's a dark bar if that's what you're worried about. Just come out for one drink." He shrugged and did his almost-smile and made what sounded like a happy moan or maybe a resigned moan, saying "Fine" or something, and, for once, he joined us.

True to its name, Harry's is huge, three or four levels. The bar on the main floor is carved in the shape of Texas and there's a big dance floor and big bright stars on the ceiling and a mechanical bull on a stage in the corner. The featured drink, sketched on a tall chalkboard, was Harry's Happy Hour Margarita in sizes large, extra large, and Sasquatch.

Bigfoot seemed to find it kind of funny, actually, and he laughed, so I ordered him one and one for myself too. The drink was huge but it seemed tiny in his claws. He drank that first margarita so fast he got a brain freeze and he roared and shook his head and laughed and reached across the bar and rang the big cowbell the bartenders play when they get a good tip.

I left him for a second to go find Lisa and by the time I came back he'd finished another and had a third in his claws. It must've hit him pretty hard because he was already a little wobbly. He took off his overcoat and his suit coat also and went out to the dance floor in his white shirt and suspenders and started dancing, one claw on his margarita, one claw pounding beats in the air.

These are the last moments anyone really remembers very clearly. Most of us blacked out at least some of it and what parts of the night anybody remembers are blurry, like bad home video. Though some details have come back to me:

Bigfoot making out with a secretary from another firm. She was blonde and had small hands that disappeared under his fur.

Bigfoot showing teeth to the bartender that tried to cut him off.

And then: Bigfoot up on the mechanical bull wearing somebody's cowboy hat and wildly swinging side-to-side, sloshing his margarita on the dancing crowd below, the whole time drunkenly roaring out all our secrets to the crowd. No one could stop him. There was stuff about alcoholics in our office, drug addicts, affairs, pornography, fraud, and a whole bunch I don't remember. "Those two," he said, pointing at us. "Those two—" and he did kisses into the air and then made with his hips like he was humping. Lisa and I were embarrassed even though we weren't even close to being the most scandalous. He just kept yelling one secret after another, everything anybody had ever told him, some secrets more comprehensible than others. Somehow he stayed upright on the bull the whole time, set a new Harry's record.

He could hardly walk once we got him down and the manager came over and asked us to leave and we helped get Bigfoot into a cab. It was only after he was gone that I realized he'd left his overcoat at the bar.

///////////

We haven't seen Bigfoot again after that night. His office went empty and the cleaning staff vacuumed up the dirt and sprayed away the smell. Every once in a while, there's a sighting around town, though these are usually second- or third-hand reports, friends at other firms saying they heard from somebody that heard from someone else that he was temping here or there. It's just the life of a temp I guess. One day you come in and they've just disappeared, recalled by the temp agency, reassigned to another firm, gone off to some other city. Bigfoot wasn't any different.

Lisa and I had to go meet with Nicholson that morning and he gave us a long speech about office relationships and keeping our careers in mind and being loyal to the firm and so on. No real punishment. But that afternoon we had a big fight that wasn't even about anything, really, and we broke up the next morning. It really hurt at the time and I went looking for Bigfoot out of muscle memory more than anything else and of course he wasn't there.

I think there was something Lisa and I had been looking for and never could find, some sort of excitement or satisfaction about what we'd made of our lives that just turned into disappointment when we tried to find it in each other. Like we thought we'd seen footprints of something special, but when we tried to make a cast of them, to preserve them, hold onto them, they filled in again with mud. Turns out the danger, the spycraft, was a big part of our attraction, and without that, neither of us was all that interested in the other; we're just two regular, boring people who work too much.

Otherwise, life at Nicholson post-Bigfoot has continued pretty much uninterrupted. We got hired onto a new case and the nights and weekends started up again. That's just the life of a law firm, too, I guess. Maybe there was some remaining whatever among the associates, but nothing we ever talked about. It was tense for a few days—not because of the secrets or Bigfoot's betrayal of our trust, but because all of a sudden we didn't know each other as well as we'd been pretending to. None of us were who we thought we were and now there was no denying it. And maybe also there was some subconscious thing we all did, some thing outside the office where we all kind of felt the need to come up with new secrets, new stories about ourselves that no one knew, just so we'd have something to be private about again.

I left Bigfoot's overcoat on the hook behind the door in the records room, which they closed up and locked after the case was over. I had forgotten all about it until I went in there this morning to file some documents I'd found in my desk, and sure enough, the coat was still there hanging. Something about it made me sad. There was some part of me, I think, that had hoped he'd come back for it, that we'd find him sneaking around the office late at night or at least that we'd find his coat gone and his tracks in the carpet, some muddy evidence he'd been back, or that he'd ever been there in the first place.

## WHAT EXISTS IN THIS DOJO

Say you've had some success in the martial arts and you're looking to run a dojo. You're a black belt. Been training for years. Decades maybe. Almost won a few small tournaments when you were younger, started making a name for yourself around Southern California. You were never quite good enough or maybe you never found out just how good you could be. Maybe there was a devastating injury; you blew out your knee mid-kick or you shattered a bone, placed the kick too low and struck your opponent's shin, the shin like concrete. Years of rehab to get back to fighting shape. It's not the same; you're not as good. You fight now with fear, with pain, with defeat. But you have a gift for teaching. You like to be called Master. And now that you've decided to be a sensei full time, there's an opening at the Cobra Kai.

Maybe you're there before class starts, get to see the kids warming up, get to scan the wall of second place trophies, silver medals. Or maybe you walk into the middle of it, the shouted instructions terse, the synchronized kicks, the repetition of it all. The class is full, every inch of mat taken up by tall blonde-haired kids named Johnny, snake-wrapped in the dojo's crisp, white, logoed karategi. There's high precision in their movement. They advance together, they retreat together, a pubescent phalanx of kicks and hi-yas. They spar in circles, attack only when ordered, like the split tongue and fangs of a cobra. They sweep the legs of the weakest. They strike first. They strike hard. They repeat: "Fear does not exist in this dojo."

In the corner, there's the man you would replace. Diamond-faced, angry, the slope of his cheeks angled down. Those who aren't his students call him Kreese. Just Kreese. Like he's at the fold of something. He has one of the Johnnies take over the class and he walks you back to his office, sits you down in an uncomfortable chair. The chair is too low, stresses your bad leg. He sees you wince, smiles. He's a man who likes to see others suffer.

First he asks you about yourself, about your interests, what brought you to karate. He asks for your references, your job history. It's more interrogation than interview. And maybe for this reason you don't tell him about the injury. Though he can sense it. He has that sense. You can read it on his lips. He smiles again and says, "Pain does not exist in this dojo." You laugh and quickly realize you weren't supposed to.

Then he tells you the history of the Cobra Kai, the philosophy, the challenge of the job. "We teach a certain strategy here, maybe different from what you know," says Kreese. "I call it the Way of the Fist. The idea is you strike first and you strike hard. You show no mercy. It's what these kids want. What their rich parents expect." He looks down. "These kids and their dirt bikes and fancy karate classes." He has a baseball bat next to his desk and he picks it up, wraps its handle into his fists. "It's what's expected of us."

This is where you say you don't understand, where he sits taller behind the desk, adopts the pose of a master, takes a breath before explaining. They say the most difficult thing in sports is hitting a round ball with a round bat. Only slightly less difficult is coiling the force of a freight train into your shoulder, uncoiling that force into the arm, into the fist, into a strike, and stopping that force cold an inch from the target. There's a certain inevitability once a strike is loaded and reversing that inevitability requires control of some equal and opposite force, some mechanism of miracles. And then to pretend like you didn't mean to, to allow yourself to be villained, to lose. "This is what it is to run the Cobra Kai dojo," he says. "As master, as sensei, you must believe that defeat does not exist in this dojo and that, in warfare, sometimes defeat is the real victory."

"But that's not karate," you say. "Karate is art and self-discipline and beauty. A physical expression of the lifelong conflict within oneself—"

"Which is exactly why we must lose," he says, his eyes wide now, and angry. "It's the only way the system works." He sits back, gets quiet.

"I was in Vietnam. Captain in the Army. You hear these stories about American soldiers burning villages. Maybe you believe them. Or maybe you believe we were right. You believe the Viet Cong were savages, that they tortured and maimed. But I was there," he says, "and I can tell you it's not that simple. You get so deep in the jungle. The heat. You forget which side you're on. You forget which side is right."

He's so quiet you have to lean in to hear and only when you're over his desk, your bad leg bent close to breaking, do you realize how vulnerable a position this is, the power of Kreese, that he could strike if he wanted. But he doesn't. "The world needs heroes. But there's no such thing as a hero without a villain. Somebody's got to be the villain. Let's be honest. It could be some earnest, rough-around-the-edges kid from New Jersey. These assholes," he says, pointing out toward the dojo floor, which is still regiment, the kids in pairs practicing unlanded sidekicks, "They're going to win at plenty of things in their lives."

Maybe this isn't your philosophy. Karate is for fun, for recreation. It's not about the fighting or the outcome. All the kids are winners. But still, you need a job. It's almost the first of the month and you haven't yet made rent. So you nod, you say, "Yeah, I get what you mean."

"Everybody wants to be a hero. That's easy. Takes a special person to be the villain." He stands and walks you back into the dojo, says, "Thanks for coming in." His handshake is firm. "You could be more menacing, but the job is yours if you want it."

This is when you stop him, before you go; you ask why he's leaving, why he's giving up on these kids who worship him. "I'm tired," he says. "Tired of losing. What we do here, we catch flies with chopsticks. And you know what? We tear off their wings and we drop them and we laugh at them and we don't have the guts to crush them. We're bullies. We're hated. And it always happens that the flies—the Daniel LaRussos—they become cranes. And we lose. Same story every time. I can't do it anymore."

Maybe you say, "I can imagine," though you probably can't, at least not yet.

And as you turn to the door, here is your decision point, the moment you have to choose. Whether fear or pain or defeat exist in your dojo. Whether your dojo can fill its black-hat role in this world. Whether your dojo is a freight train that can stop in its tracks, a coil that can be both sprung and, an instant later, unsprung, a strike that's never struck. Whether your dojo can be a villain. The question isn't whether you're strong enough to win. But whether you're strong enough to lose.

Maybe you turn to him and say, "I'll do it." Or maybe you're afraid of the job, the challenge. Maybe you still want to be a hero. Maybe you think it's easier to be a hero. And so instead you turn toward the door, walk back out into the blaze of the sun and say, "I'll let you know."

# WILLOW

Now she used the scarves as tourniquets, here on the floor of the rented house. Their cotton fibers seemed stronger from the tie-dye and, from the strong cinch of them, the bottom half of her was turning purple and cold. It was a method she'd read about, a last ditch sort of thing, this corporal idea of divide and conquer, and she focused her breathing as much as she could focus and as much as she could breathe, which wasn't much and not deep, on resisting the clawing pain inside. This disease that was eating her alive. These scarves that had once held her hair. It was darker then, her hair, a deep brown that Arlo called chestnut. It wasn't until a dozen or so years later hiking the Appalachian that she actually saw the tree and decided he was wrong. Yes, the color was close, though hers was a richer brown. But there was something severe about the tree that didn't match and she'd always thought of herself more as a free cascade of furls, like a willow. That was the whole reason she'd borrowed that name for most of those years; if anyone asked, she'd simply smile and untie her scarves and twirl her long hair free on the wind. Now it was gray and unmoving.

This was supposed to have been a place of positive energy, this specific spot, this house a vortex, and she'd offered all she had left to stay in this big empty, of which she'd used so little. The waste of it all. She hadn't really moved from this space at the center of the floor since coming here. She'd watched the seasons from here, felt the desert press up through the floorboards, tried to absorb its pulse. When she could still stand, she would maybe go to the kitchen to make tea and also there were the cactus fruits that grew out back that she would eat. She could feel the vitamins and minerals moving through her, fighting to unclench the pain's fist. It seemed so strong, somehow stronger than she'd ever been. She regretted the violence of it.

The scarves weren't working. She could feel nails scratching past the boundary up into the all of her. She pulled at the scarves again with her skeleton-white arms until they wouldn't tighten any more, watched the bottom of her fade. Funny that the things she thought of now were things she'd tried so hard not to remember. The day she left home when she was a girl. Her first trip. There was that morning, also, after she and the others had leaped onto a freight in the dark, and then later in the open car with the sun rising and the freight pushing through the sand mountains of California and the sun painting the mountains purple, the majesty of it that made her understand that song. Her decirculating body now purpling like those mountains, and like the mountains, passing behind her.

She reached for another scarf and drew it, best she could, across her chest, cinched it against her ribs to save her heart. *It's the only thing I've ever needed*, she thought. She thought also about calling her brother. They hadn't talked in so long. She hadn't seen him since their mother's funeral. He was in a suit that day, tried to split things with her in the name of their mother, like a person's life could be split, like the things left behind are what matter. There was his whole talk about her taking responsibility for once and how she'd be helped by it. Then, she'd resolved not to be helped because she wanted to be unburdened by possessions. Now, she'd resolved not to call for help as a last promise to herself not to burden others with this, to pass, if she was to pass, without leaving a trace.

Still, there was part of her—probably the diseased part, she thought, the gripping scorpions of pain under her skin, stinger tails cocked and jabbing—that didn't want to die alone, and for that reason, she tried to let herself cry. She closed her eyes to the morning, forced them closed, tried to force tears. Except she couldn't. She realized then too that her mouth was dry. She felt the desert vortex opening, crossing her over. And that's when the last image came, not a crossing, but a dispersing. Her body like a mandala that was now being swept away in the tornadoing sand. And this made her smile, the purity of this thought: that all of this was just giving it back, returning what she borrowed.

## A MONSTER FOR ALWAYS

That night there were frostquakes and thundersnow and the whole house shook and swayed like bombs were falling, like an army was down the street clearing houses the way we've seen in movies. In fact, out the front window we saw cop lights, blue and red swivels patrolling the neighborhood, looking, we guessed, for the Snow Man we were hiding in the shed out back.

Meghan said, "If they come to our house we can't say anything because they'll take him away from us and do all sorts of tests on him." We were in the front sitting room we never used, ducked below the windowsill, and only every once in a while sat up to look out.

I said, "I know," and looked to see whether the police car had turned down our street. He had, and I ducked again under the red and then the blue as the lights took turns crossing through the window.

"They think he's a monster," she said. That's what the papers were calling him, anyway—the Snow Monster. But really he was just a man, or at least an animal no different from a bear or our dog, Sitka, and we'd never call Sitka a monster unless she'd get into the garbage while we were at the store or out to dinner. Even then, she was just impatient and wanted us to get home and you can't really blame something for needing its people.

Meghan and I were out in the forest near our house when we found him. It's not a big forest—just a square block in the middle of our subdivision—but when you're in it, it seems like it goes for miles. The trees were all bare and sickly and there were thin trails of white snow piled on the branches from the last time it had snowed. School was off and we'd decided we wanted to make a movie that day. We'd thought up a story about two adventurers lost out in the middle of a big woods and making all sorts of discoveries. The trees there are all pretty thick, and I was trying to shake the trunks to make the snow fall, to make it look like it was snowing for the camera. But it wasn't working; they were too thick to move.

Meghan kept filming anyway, and that's when she shouted, "Holy shit, Sean, there's a great big something behind you."

We were afraid at first and he was too—he roared something fierce—but he looked nice enough and I whispered, "We won't hurt you," and that seemed to calm him. He figured out what we were trying to do with the tree and he stood off-camera and shook it for us and it started snowing just like for real.

It was one of the best movies we've ever made.

He followed us home and we showed him the shed. Mom never went in there after Dad left, and it was supposed to be cold that night, so Meghan said, "You can stay here whenever you like, just make sure nobody sees you."

He reached out toward her with his big white paw, maybe to shake her hand or something, but she gave him her head and he patted it softly. He had snow on his claws and some of it melted on her. Water dripped down her face and I laughed. He was the first big thing we'd met in a while that was nice to us without wanting something back.

Anyway, at some point walking around the neighborhood the next day, he must've been spotted, because somebody called the cops and there was a whole big thing about him on the news. Meghan and I went out to the shed to see him and he was feeling pretty bad about being seen. I think he thought he'd really screwed up.

"It's okay," she said. "It'll all be okay. There's nothing time can't fix," which was a thing Dad used to say. "But you better stay in here. People are looking for you."

And that was the night of the frostquakes. Mom said it happens when the moisture in the soil freezes and starts to expand and it cracks the earth, just like a real quake. Except it sounded more like explosions, and then there were the booms of the thundersnow too, and the whole night was just scarier than anything.

Meghan said, "Don't worry. I'll take care of you," which was something Mom had said that afternoon, though now she was out on a date with some guy from her work and told us not to expect her until late. Still, I was worried, less about Meghan and me and more about Mom. The street looked tough to drive on. There was snow coming down and I knew there was a sheet of ice under the snow. I thought she might have a hard time getting back to us.

The cop car was going slow, and over an hour or two, he must have passed our house three times. Each time, the fallen snow banked taller. And then we just happened to be watching on the fourth time he was coming around the corner. Except he did it a little too fast and his back wheels slipped and the back of his car went spinning into a tall bank of snow at the end of our driveway. He revved the engine and it roared like the Snow Man. Smoke came up from the tires he was gunning it so hard. But the car wouldn't budge. He stopped, and it looked like he was trying to get out but his door was blocked by the snow.

I hadn't realized Meghan wasn't next to me while I was watching this, and when I looked over to the front door, she already had her jacket on and was putting on her boots.

"We wouldn't be much help," I said. "We can't push a car out of the snow."

She said, "I know," and then went through the house toward the back door. I put my boots on and followed her out across the yard to the shed. The Snow Man was there, asleep on the air mattress we'd blown up and left for him.

Meghan told him about the police car, about how the cop was trapped inside and how no one else was home who could help. "It'll be dangerous," she said. "But we're supposed to help when people are in trouble and Mom's still out there. And maybe if you do it they'll see you're not a monster."

As soon as she said it, I think we all realized it wasn't true. Once they decide you're a monster, you're a monster for always.

Even so, he was out of the shed before she finished talking, out around the side of the house. He was faster than us, better at walking through the snow, and when we got to the front yard, he was already in the street pushing the car out of the snow bank. The cop looked scared even after he saw what was going on, and he had his gun out inside the car. There was a loud frostquake then, a loud whipcrack just as the Snow Man pushed the car loose. The cop's foot was still on the accelerator and the car leaped forward down the street with the snow still falling and the Snow Man in the rearview mirror running in the opposite direction down the street, back toward the forest.

A minute or two later, the cop had the car turned around and he headed toward the forest, after the Snow Man, with his lights on and swiveling red and blue through the neighborhood.

Then the street was empty again. The quakes kept going and so did the thunder and the snow kept falling, like maybe the thunder was just shaking the snow from the clouds and the ground underneath us was shifting from the weight of it all. There wasn't a moon that night and it would've been pitch dark except for all the fresh snow, which made it seem like a different kind of dark, lighter somehow. Meghan and I stayed outside for a while waiting for Mom and scooping snow with our bare hands and squeezing it into tight fist-shaped bricks until the bricks melted between our fingers or our hands got too cold, all the while thinking if her car slipped on the ice, monster or no monster, we could at least try to help.

## THE RUST BELT

She was tired of people asking where she's from. It was a question, she'd decided, that was both too strange and too familiar. There were any number of details that would say more about her. Her favorite dessert, for example, or the make of her first car. But still the question of her hometown came up more than she thought should be usual. In supermarkets. At conferences. During chance encounters with strangers on the street. She began to hold up her hand before the question was out. At first she meant this to say "Michigan" but then later to mean "Stop." Sometimes she'd stick her hands into her pockets and say "The Midwest," which wasn't specific. Or other times she'd say "The Suburbs," which was even less specific but also very specific in important ways that few people understood.

She found if she chose not to answer, they'd try to fill in her blanks. There were some who saw her and said "Farm Girl." Some would say "City Girl." And when she had the energy and the patience she'd say, "No, but not no." This in-between. This question. It was like trying to know someone by skin alone. And there was so much more to her, wasn't there? So much more to everyone than where they're from.

Although, there was this: a small patch of flesh on her back, behind her breast, between the wing of the trapezius and the sharp creases of scapula. This small patch in a shape she could not name—something rhombic—and that, whenever she'd travel, would glow warm through the threads of her shirt, burning a bright brown-orange grit graveling deeper and deeper within her the farther she journeyed from home.

## LEGEND OF LINK AND Z

Zelda had a scam she'd run sometimes where she'd have Link push her into traffic, out in front of a moving car. This wasn't something she could do on her own—she needed Link for that last loose force she couldn't control, wouldn't have to will. If they timed it right, the driver would slam on his brakes just a little too late and she'd hit the hood and sometimes she'd roll up onto the windshield and be flung off when the car stopped. She'd be wearing a fake belly under her dress and she'd cry and tell the driver she was pregnant and she couldn't feel the baby. Link would run in like the concerned father, his green tunic all sweat-soaked and shaking. And together they'd con the driver into handing over whatever he had in his pocket. Sometimes cab fare to get to the hospital or to get home. Sometimes, if it was a fancy car and if Link could sell it, they'd get the driver thinking they were going to call one of those slip-and-fall guys from the TV and the driver'd better pay up before it becomes a whole thing.

It was never very much money and there were only so many times they could get away with it in any one city. So they moved around a lot, hitchhiking wherever trucks would take them. New York and Philadelphia and DC. Winters, they'd try to get to the coast and get south because she liked the sun and the ocean, liked to sit out on the beach while Link would busk. Sword tricks on the boardwalks for whatever bits of change he could get people to drop. Sometimes he'd play his ocarina.

For a while Zelda had a thing where she wanted to be an actress and so Link bought them bus tickets for as far west as they could afford, which wasn't far, and they hitched the rest of the way. Except LA wasn't how the movies made it look and Zelda got bored fast. "I just don't feel like playing their game anymore," she said one morning after another failed audition. They were sitting under the pier eating funnel cakes Link had bought with money he'd lifted out of a wallet some surfer left on the beach. Lazy waves lapped over their feet.

"Z, it's warm all year here. We can stay here and be comfortable."

She didn't smile, didn't even look at him. "There's something more for us. Just not here."

This was a thing Zelda would say a lot, that there was something better beyond wherever they were. Like there was some castle she could see in the distance that she thought she and Link could reach, somewhere they belonged. But the castle kept moving, shifting, and however hard or fast they moved toward it, it never came closer, always stood just over the horizon, just out of focus.

They spent the rest of that spring headed back east and, by Link's compass, north. He didn't tell her but he'd read about Detroit and was inching them there. A city of abandoned buildings where anyone could make a home out of nothing. Sometimes when he got sad that's all he could imagine they'd ever have: nothing. Other times, usually late at night or when they hadn't eaten in a few days and were feeling light-headed, Zelda would lay down next to him, her head on his chest, and grab his hand.

Zelda's scam didn't work well in Detroit. There weren't many fancy cars not worn over with rust, and whenever they'd try to run it, most of the time the driver'd just shrug his shoulders, get back into his car, and drive off. Sometimes the driver would offer to take her to the hospital or to his home, to his family. His wife was a nurse, maybe, or maybe he had some extra food or could put Link and Zelda up for a night, just to make sure their fake baby was okay.

But Link had found them a place to sleep at the edge of the city, a house with its insides carved out. They spread out their packs and made a bed. Zelda hung a painting she'd made as a kid. And they took in the wild dog they found one morning digging through the weeds out back. Link figured there wasn't any trash for him to eat, that there has to be something worth something and then something left over before there could even be trash. They fed him when they could. And when it started to get cold and ice started freezing up through the floorboards, they spent nights pulled into each other with the dog between them or on top of them or at their feet.

There was that night it snowed like it'd never stop. Link kept hold of her hand until morning.

And it was sometime after that first snow that Zelda flinched. They were downtown at the corner of Woodward and Gratiot, and Link put his hands on the small of her back and went to push her forward like always, except this time she pressed back against him. He didn't get the idea at first and tried again, pushed her harder so she couldn't resist and she stumbled headlong into the path of a Buick that hit a patch of ice and came in heavier than she was used to, heavier than she was expecting.

They spent that night in the hospital with the guy from the Buick. His wife came down later and brought them soup and sandwiches and rolls. Link held some back, put a roll in the pocket of his tunic to take to the dog if the dog was still there whenever they got home. Zelda went in for surgery around ten and Link found a quiet spot in the hallway to wait, stood there all night staring at the wall, memorizing the map posted on it, the rooms and paths of the hospital, all the different ways in and out.

## OLD PLYMOUTH

I always told him our Dad's old Plymouth'd break down just in the last place at the last minute he'd want. When he was far away from something or on his way to somewhere. And there my brother was when they found him, side of the interstate halfway between everywhere, frozen dead, hands all chewed up by work or wolves or God knows, eyes still on the road, looking out through the cracked front glass. Probably watching the fall of the ice drops, watching them shatter against the asphalt, melt cool for a half-second, and freeze up again like nothing, like they were always part of the earth and had always been here.

The cops called me away from my Sunday bacon and waffles to come identify the body, and still it took half a day's drive with the four-wheel flipped. County morgue hadn't even made it out yet and he's sitting there looking like the last time I threw him out of my house. Colder. More gray. His eyes'd gone to blue crystals in the middle, frost on the forehead scar from when Dad cracked him one big, and his hat was turned off-center. Otherwise, wasn't anything different I could tell. Body guys from the morgue showed up not too much later and lifted him up real gentle. He came out whole and seated, all in one solid piece, and they put him in their truck that way. Laid him on his back like an astronaut. Don't think they had the heart to crack his legs straight in front of me but they didn't know I'd already pictured it ten times, and in my ears, it was the only sound I could hear.

Trooper called him a hypotherm, said he'd probably been there since one, maybe midnight. Said once they go stiff, sometimes you can revive them, sometimes you can't. Especially tough if they're already "depleted," was the word he used. Nearest hospital in the next county. Nothing out here but trees. Not too many cars make this stretch of road at night, he said. And the ones that do usually know in all that snow they don't stop for anything. A car stops out here, the road's so slick, it might not get started again.

The one thing that bothered me is I'll never know what he was up to. Can't think where he would've been going so late, what it was so urgent got him out in that mess of a car. Woman maybe. Or a fix. Or worse. Road he was on doesn't lead anywhere. I know. I drove it. After all the county people left. Got in my pickup and took it all the way to the lake. Dead ends at a put-in. All the way, trees were frozen. Road's frozen. Put-in's frozen. Lake's frozen. Whatever's on the other side, frozen. Ice to ice, my brother.

And there's nothing to do with all that frozen but keep wondering. Made me wonder like we did when we were kids. Growing up in the north woods with the cold and the dark and the afternoon grays. We'd make up stories, pretend we were somewhere we weren't. I did it that night. In bed, looking up at the ceiling, thought about his body like that, like maybe he meant it, like he really was ready to top a tall rocket. And just for a minute, I turned on my back, too, and pulled my knees up to my chest, frozen ghost of him there next to me, both of us lifting off all the way into space. Probably the least lonely either of us had been in a long while. Closest we've ever been to stars, too.

## THE ALLEGORY OF THE BOXER AND THE SPY

Before there were countries, there were two rival towns at opposite ends of an empire, both towns on coasts and between them a countryside of plains and mountains and waterways. They were the only towns in the empire, and over the years the towns grew into small cities with neighborhoods and downtowns and then into bigger cities with suburbs and airports and networks of highways within and around. Barons built long railroads and telephone lines across the empire, too, but these tracks and roads and wires were little used.

Ask anyone in either town when the war started and they'd probably say what the textbooks say—that nobody remembers the start of it, but certainly there must have been a time when the empire aspired to be whole and the two towns were friendly. There must have been a time, they'd say, when the countryside meant opportunity and hope, a time before the two towns were sides and the middle was rendered a battlefield, before all the checkpoints and the papers and the uniforms. Surely, sometime in the country's past, they'd say, families must have traveled freely, and children grew up and left one town for the other for school or for work or for love.

Both towns chose their own leaders who, in theory, shared power over the empire, though many of these leaders were elected on promises they'd protect their town from the impositions of the other. Each town hired police to safeguard its streets against the other and they both raised armies to stand guard on their borders and they cultivated sources and informants and spies to keep watch on the other town, to keep even, to make sure their town didn't fall behind in technology, industry, and other things.

One year, the empire experienced a drought, the worst drought they'd ever known. Citizens of both towns prayed for rain, and after too many waterless months, the situation got desperate. Crops failed and people starved. They grew weak and mad. There were riots and looting and pleas for imperial unity to resolve the crisis. Elections were called and reformers swept into office. The new leaders agreed to meet for a railway summit, and they conducted negotiations in a rail car while crisscrossing the empire.

Somewhere near the top of a mountain, the leaders struck a framework for peace and an outline for the long process of reconciliation. As they signed the deal, the conductor blew a celebratory train whistle and the porters poured champagne. And in a show of goodwill, the towns scheduled a boxing match, a fair and friendly competition between the towns' best fighters. In its civility, a metaphor for renewed relations.

The leaders commissioned a stadium on a low, flat, neutral acreage near the center of the empire. Coaches were chosen and boxers in each town were invited to tryouts where all of their skills were measured, their physical attributes assessed, and their intangibles tested, intangibles like grit and determination and resilience.

That summer, each coach put his boxer through workouts and drills and sparring matches. And both towns, without telling the other, activated their networks of spies to learn all they could about the other fighter. Reports from these spies were comprehensive. There were details on each boxer's strengths and weaknesses, his speed and agility, his past fights, his tendencies in the ring, his training regimen, his coach, his eating and grooming habits, his love life. The content of this intelligence was uncanny. If you had compared both reports before the fight, you could only have concluded that the two boxers were perfectly matched. There was no reason for the fight to result in anything other than a draw.

The towns organized miles-long parades to deliver their boxers to the fight, parades of floats and marching bands and caged animals and giant balloons. The seldom-used highways bustled with the traffic of cars and buses and RVs, all bound for the new stadium.

The day of the fight, there was a storm so strong it tore flags from poles, toppled trees, and turned the fields around the stadium to mud. The townspeople rejoiced. They drank the rain and played in the fields. The rain was forecast to continue for days, but it cleared temporarily in the evening. There was a last burst of sun before dark, and the leaders of the towns arrived and took their seats in a shared suite overlooking the ring.

The fight was everything that night. Anyone who wasn't at the stadium gathered in bars or town squares to watch the broadcast. Celebrity guest announcers introduced the boxers, and an impartial referee was flown in from a neighboring empire. The boxers shook hands, and, together, the oldest citizens of each town rang the bell.

The boxers danced out from their corners and circled for a good ten seconds before the first punch was thrown, a left-hand jab followed quickly by a right hook. Both blows were blocked. An uppercut connected. A second jab popped the guy in the forehead. A hook landed, and then another uppercut, and the one boxer's head flopped to the side and got caught by another hook. He staggered backward and collapsed in a diagonal. Thirty-nine seconds into the fight, it was over. Some in the crowd booed.

Stories about the fight occupied much of the column space in the next day's papers. One headline declared its town superior, celebrated the victory they all expected. The other described it as an unthinkable loss. And even now, with the memory of the fight firmly in the history of the former empire, now a country, there are some in the one town who insist the fight was fixed, that their boxer was a plant—a spy working in service of the opposing town. Others believe the pre-match reports were faulty, that there's no way in a fight so fair the victory could have been so decisive. Strength doesn't work that way. The theory goes that if you could look into the towns' records from that year, still sealed in the country's secret archives, you'd see both boxers were spies, their histories fabricated, and that one spy was simply better at fighting than the other.

What the wisest in both towns would say, though: no matter the accuracy or amount of information in a forecast, no matter the weatherman's skill or preparation, no matter the cloud's size or its strength. Some days, the rain pours like they say. And some days, not a plea or a prayer can make fall a single drop.

## TONTO RIDES A BUS TO VISIT HIS MOTHER-IN-LAW WHO IS DYING FROM CANCER

### 1

He'd asked his ex for Oreos from the vending machine, and she'd left him there alone in the room. The stiff chair and the polished, gray-flecked floor. And the rest: the impossible whiteness of it all. The walls and bed linens and curtains and stuff. Everything bleached white and sharp. Alone, except not alone. There was the beeping monitor and also the edges and folds of the white sheets, the fluid lines running to her veins, needles disappearing under skin.

### 2

He woke in the middle of the country somewhere—everywhere passing in the summer dark looking like every other where passing in the summer dark: black and sweaty. There was a knock against his shoulder, the nylon of a bag against his face, his face pressed harder into the bus glass, a "Sorry," and then a new man next to him, next to the plastic divider. He was there all the way to Detroit.

Before that, there was the kid that sat down even though he'd set his bag on the empty seat, spread himself out to make it look taken. The kid asked him to move it and then went right to sleep. He'd had to hold it for a while, through a whole state at least, until finally he convinced himself to speak. He cleared his throat and there wasn't any response, said "sorry but can I" and nothing, raised his voice, asked the kid if he'd let him out to use the bathroom in the back. But the kid was out—probably drunk, he thought—and the overfull feeling lasted until the scheduled stop and then it was still a few minutes until the aisle was clear and he could get to the back.

And then there was the half-sleep in which he dreamed about something he'd forgotten as soon as he woke up. All he remembered was that the dream was intense and there were other people in it that he'd known before but hadn't talked to in a few years, hadn't even seen.

## 3

He'd always thought of his breath as iodine and once looked up the root of the word: Greek, meaning violet or purple. It sounded right to him. More than that, he thought of himself as a helper, someone who heals others' wounds. There are people, he'd thought, who live for themselves. And there are people who live for others, and maybe that was why she'd called him and asked him to come. Called him like nothing after their however many years apart. He thought it'd be a good chance to see the boys, let them meet him, but she didn't respond to that email. And the bus was a few hours later than scheduled and she wasn't there at the station so he took a cab that cost all the cash he had, the meter going while the cab crossed out from the mess of downtown and into the suburbs, to the hospital. It looked like a castle, taller and more royal and more defensible than others he'd been in.

## 4

His ex-mother-in-law had never thought of him as real family. Told him so every time they met. The divorce was some kind of validation. Now it was his ex who wasn't sure. Since he arrived, it was "stay with her," "hold her hand," "touch her forehead," "say something curing." Like he's some sort of medicine man. He just wanted to ask for his cab fare back. "I don't think you understand," he said. "That's not what I—" And then the doctor came in. He said they'd tried everything, that the only things left were whatever goodbyes.

She yelled at him to do it, yelled over his saying, "I don't know how. I'm not—"

She said, "You've never understood what she means to us. Just...please."

## 5

And then the Oreos. There was the bank of outlets near the floor at the side of the bed. He figured there had to be some failsafe to the machines in case of power outage or whatever. No way simply unplugging would do anything. Maybe it'd stop the monitor, erase evidence of a heart he'd never seen. But she wouldn't die from it. There was a whole procedure—he'd looked it up before he left—legal documents, religious things, stop the respirator, choke out the tubes.

He reached for the power cords, pulled at them half-heartedly. There wasn't any give. They were secure in their sockets and it was all the resistance he needed. Though there was part of him that thought it would've been nice just to be alone for a couple minutes.

She came back with the cookies and he took them and said, "I'd like to see the boys before I go." It was afternoon and they'd be on their way home from school, he thought. Probably there was a nanny waiting for them, maybe their stepfather. Whatever, he felt some right to it, to be with them. And when she said no, he wanted to hit her but didn't. Instead, he said, "Stop me."

She tried but he pushed past her, his hand on her shoulder, still gentle but firmer now. Back down to the lobby of the hospital. Stopped at the ATM, at the gift shop.

In the round drive there was a line of cabs waiting. He hired one, and as he ducked to get in and as he closed the door, there was something about it that felt like mounting a horse. He had a feeling then of riding out across the plains toward the sun and who knows where else.

# BETWEEN

# THE DEAD DREAM OF BEING UNDEAD

## Part I

Once, there were two brothers born nine months apart in the same room of the same hospital in the same manner—the protracted period of ill-timed contractions, the doctor in blue scrubs and white mask, the late-night crowning, the father's kiss, the death of the mother. And with each child's arrival and each mother's passing, the father celebrated and mourned in the only way he'd ever learned to do either: asleep in the arms of a new woman. Christenings were funerals. Cradles were made altars.

Not until their tenth year on a day four and one-half months after the oldest's birthday and four and one-half months before the youngest's birthday did the father reveal to the boys they weren't borne of the same woman and that the woman they'd known as their mother was in fact mother to neither. And it wasn't until this day in their tenth year that either brother had considered the differences between them, had even recognized there were differences between them other than their nine months' difference in age.

But these differences, once noticed by the brothers, seemed to them both fateful. That the oldest brother thought in shapes and in waves, the youngest brother in numbers and formulae. That the youngest brother had fingers that were thin and tapered and the oldest had hands that were meatlike and gnarled. That the oldest brother was brown haired and fast growing while the youngest brother wore blonde at the height of his pale flat body. That his young face was flat and round, while the oldest brother's was sharp and angular like an adze. That the oldest was born out of an expression of pure ecstatic love between the father and the first mother, the youngest of something else—love, sure, for the second mother, but also grief probably, or bereavement.

These differences in character, which some called distinctive, the brothers called separating and shattering. Like until this time they'd been faces on either side of a mirror, only now recognizing the other's reflection as a mimic, only now realizing this glass between them wasn't a mirror at all. And the oldest and the youngest each wondered, then, whether he was the one on the other side, on the outside, alone in the cold, staring in through this imagined window.

In their house there was a real window, a window in the room they shared, and at night this window became a portal to the world outside. "Are you awake?" the youngest would ask the oldest. "Yes, but you shouldn't be," the oldest would answer. "You should go to sleep." "Why do I have to sleep when you won't sleep?" the youngest would ask. "Because I'm older and I said so," the oldest would answer.

And they would continue in this way, the way brothers do, with the youngest brother asking questions—about the father, about his work and about the window and the city beyond, about their mothers, about those nine months in which one brother was alive and the other was not, about the first mother and the second mother, neither of whom he was alive to know. He asked about how people die and what it means to be dead. "Dead just means you're not alive anymore," the oldest brother would say. "So dead isn't forever?" the youngest would ask, and the oldest would answer, "It is. Probably. Nobody really knows. Forever hasn't happened yet."

Beginning late those nights in their tenth year, the brothers began to explore the world outside their family home. The youngest brother would pull himself through the window, slowly lower to the level below, gain a foothold on the frame of the kitchen window, and softly launch himself the last feet to the ground, careful to avoid the protruding roots of the maple that towered over their backyard. In the dark, the youngest brother investigated the fauna of the night, the owls and earthworms and foxes and bats that stalked the yards of all the children in the neighborhood. He stood in the middle the yard, licked his finger, and raised it to measure the force and the direction of the wind. He braced himself against the bank of their low-running backyard creek and dipped his toes to measure the depth and the temperature of the water. The creek was murky, strewn with rocks, and lumbering. It raged only occasionally, often in spring after the snowmelt, but most nights it lay slow and quiet as the rest of the sleeping neighborhood.

The oldest brother, too, would pull himself into the frame of the same bedroom window. He would leap wildly to a near branch of the maple and swing himself to the tree's trunk and shimmy to the ground, stripping bark and skin, absorbing splinters and surfacing blood. Except his night wanderings weren't confined to the yard. In his tenth and eleventh and twelfth years, he rode out into the night on his bicycle; in later years, he ran; in later years, he rolled the family Plymouth backward and silent down the driveway and at the bottom of the driveway, turned the engine softly and drove a block before charging the headlamps. At first, this was all for exploration, then for adventure and thrill, then to meet friends who were expecting him and who he wanted to please, then for things he couldn't do near the house, things that could only be done in the unwatched parts of the night city. He liked discovering places that had been abandoned by others. They became his spaces. They became places he was free to do anything he wanted, like smoke or hide.

As a family, they measured time not in days or in weeks but in the father's shifts and in pay periods. The father worked on a factory line, most often the day shift but sometimes the swing shift and sometimes the night.

The factory ceilings were tall and corrugated and the floor was long and poured in gray cement tracked with yellow lines. Behind this there was a chaos of machinery. Steel was forged with pulleys and levers and pincers and gears, all of it bright and loud in its chrome and massive, a moving mass whose workings made sense only to the men who, like the father, had been there longest. They were, themselves, machinery, their movements critical to completing a process bigger than any one of them. Newer men only knew their own stations, their own specific tasks. These new men knew the cars they helped make as half-assembled strips of steel and pipes and blocks and steering columns, cars that couldn't start because there were not yet keys.

Whatever shift, whatever phase of the sun or moon the father could see through the factory window, the work was tedious. He had survived two wives and worked to support a third, and still the repetition and din of the factory would grind at his bones if he let it. Every morning as he left the third wife asleep in their bed, he would steel himself, stiffen his body against the day to come. And every night as he drove the freeway home, he would have to release it, the tension of the day that had passed.

With age, it had become harder to steel himself, harder to know when to steel himself. Everything had become harder, at home with the third wife and the brothers and at work with the foreman and on the freeway in between. Other cars passed faster than seemed safe. Some days he felt invisible and other days he steeled himself so completely he felt skinless, bloodless, and chrome, like he was only steel.

One night after supper, in his chair and switching channels on the television, his stomach wrenched and twisted. He felt his stomach harden. He poked at it and saw stars shooting. He couldn't breathe and he slid to the floor. He woke for a moment under hospital lights on a metal operating table, doctors and nurses protected by gloves and masks and working inside him, no different from the men in the factory. In the moment he was awake, he wondered how it would feel to have a factory inside him, to have embedded within him the twisted, wrenching steel of the line. The next moment he was out again.

He woke repaired, but frail and penetrable. The third wife made him swear he'd protect himself. And as soon as he was allowed, he returned to his place in the factory, up and running again on the factory line. At work, he began to wear shin pads and kneepads, a fire shirt and a smock. He wore plugs to protect his ears and goggles to protect his eyes and the sight and the sound of the loud factory floor was muted to him because of it, the factory floor taking on the tone of a trumpet and the colors of early spring—not the pastel pinks and blues and greens, but the soft shades of gray the sky would sometimes turn, the funnel streaks of white from the factory smokestacks that pressed up into the gray clouds as through sewer grates. Winter was a low shade of cold blue, and the areas outside the factory where the father would stand with a cigarette and a handkerchief during breaks adopted the flat, grainy colors of old home movies.

For the father, it was comfortingly familiar. This life behind goggles, between earplugs, reminded him of times before the hard deaths of the women he'd loved, before he came to fear for this new woman, this third wife, to fear he may have some lingering death in the tips of his fingers and that soon there would be, there would have to be, the death of this woman, too. And then, inevitably, the deaths of these two brothers, these two boys who looked like him in different lights, who sounded like him in different words, who were like him and like their mothers. These brothers his last remaining alive relation to the women he'd lost.

Maybe for this reason, he began to see life at the ends of shifts—life at home—the same as the factory. Too bright and too loud, too sharp in contrast and timbre. And so he began to wear the earplugs and the eye goggles at home, thinking that if he kept all life muted and dim, if he kept from reacting to his family world too harshly or too excitedly or too gravely or too anything, he might be able to spare these six happy eyes that greeted him each evening at the head of the driveway, these six eyes no longer blue and green and hazel, but safe gray.

On drives home up the interstate, he had to adjust for new blind spots. He found there were spaces at his sight's edge that held hazards— speeding cars or potholes or road debris, thrown-off remnants of past crashes or flung treads from the tires of Mack trucks. He could no longer hear horns in anything other than dim waves.

Dinners were the same, his ovoid vision at the kitchen table restricted to one brother at a time if he chose to look at the brothers or to his wife if he chose to look at his wife or to his food if he chose to look at his food and, because of this, meals were more intimate somehow. Shower water became white noise and particle falls in the fog. Before laying down to sleep, he would stretch the strap of the goggles and scratch at the band-shaped impression on the back of his head, try to invert the impression left in his thinning brown hair.

In the pre-sleep dark, his third wife would tell him about her recipes, her friends, her day, tell him her fears and her dreams, anything. Any topic it seemed to her they should talk about. The father had trouble identifying the shapes of these words, the shapes between them, the pauses between the ebbs and flows of her lilts and furls. But he felt in her brass tone and the soft tilt of her hips that she'd press toward him, against him, the only words he could imagine her ever meaning: "I desperately want a child that is all ours, only ours, only us. I would prefer a girl, though another son would do." And every night he pressed her back, away.

She threatened to leave once. He watched as she took her coat and her hat and stood near the door. He stopped her, held her close, let her feel the stretch of his goggles against her ear and the hard wheeze of his chest pleading for her not to go. She said she loved him and she loved the brothers like sons and for those reasons she would stay.

There was the day at the factory the winch pulled and the line sped up. Parts of cars came swinging around faster than normal. Robotic arms charging the full weight of steel along the tracks in the floor like mad bulls in a ring, the faces of the men bright red in the scrambling. There was a loud grinding noise.

The father, with his bolt gun and oil sprayer, adjusted without thinking, slotting bolts in chassis undersides faster and with sharper aim, with shorter and more brusque fits of motion. These muscles that were once his own and that had been changed by this factory floor, muscles that during his years here had settled into the soft flow of assembly line movement, their twitching fiber gears ground. These movements that had become engrained in him, but that had become long and laconic in the everyday repetition of the same task. Some days before this one, he thought of himself as conducting a symphony or banking a plane or a boat, swinging his arms through a fastball—some job that was not his, some life that was not his. Now with the speedup, these movements sharpened again, had to sharpen again, and the father again found in his muscles the precision that had brought him here in the first place, the unusual mind for perfection that had gotten him the job. This sharp sense of things he thought lost, or, at least, that had evaporated into ether, into a smell maybe but otherwise into nothingness. Suddenly, the sense returned and for the first time he could remember since the birth of the oldest son, he smiled.

Others on the factory floor weren't as quick to recover and the line swiftly swung free from order into confusion. Ratchets got caught in the machinery. Broken bodies began to stack at line's end. The plant's welders threw off tall spiking sparks from the tips of their torches, sparks that spat from the air and lit workshirt cotton. There were crushes of metal and language, orders, directions, flattened under the wincing scream of twisting and scraping. Busted, jagged metal falling in torn sheets and pilings. Warning lights flashed, alarms sounded, bright and guttural and acid and overwhelming, like at once they'd turned on all the lamps and horns at the front ends of these cars they were meant to assemble.

The father didn't hear or see any of this. There was just, in his mind, under cover of the plugs and goggles, the grainy crackling light and soft awe like the night the oldest son was made. The squint of the first wife. The electric tall of the soft short hairs of her skin. The soft leather of the bench seat of the Plymouth. The Independence Day fireworks.

He woke from this dream on the cold cement ground of the factory smothered under a fire blanket and the weight of the shift foreman. His goggles and plugs had come off in the tackle, and he could see and hear it all now. He could hear the men yelling, "Everybody out! Everybody out!" He could feel the sharp, singing pain of burnt flesh on his forearms, on his neck, his back. The way his legs moved slower and stiffer than he knew they should.

The outside was new and hard as well, and without thinking he pulled backward from the flame of his lighter, couldn't bring it close enough, hard as he tried, to light the end of a cigarette. And so he just stood there with the others, watched firemen douse the flames, watched smoke and steam escape the factory in apocalyptic, cloudlike bursts that floated faster and more wildly than earlier days' straight smokestack plumes.

No one knew the cause for sure. Around the pool tables of the bar across the street, some of the men assumed it was conspiracy. The union contract had expired and the company was taking a hard line. Maybe the company saw a slowdown coming and had been speeding up the line a little at a time over some weeks as a way of increasing productivity and piling some backstock without paying for extra shifts. This event, the story went, was the unexpected end of their means, a catastrophe that was nothing more than everything they deserved.

After the second round of pitchers, others of the men started thinking maybe it was sabotage, that maybe this was one man's or several men's attempt at persuasion, in which case "I didn't see or hear nothing" and "I'm not one to say" is what each man said in turn.

The father, his arms wrapped and his other burns salved but stinging, was maybe the only man who actually didn't know or didn't want to know. He had his own idea. Different from the other men, he saw something more meaningful and calamitous in the day. The sparks and the steel and the smoke. The smoldering factory remains. The untenable mechanisms of machines and industry. He saw them all as legends on a large map, an atlas of the end of times.

And at home that night, he went to the basement and reached up above the dust-covered top of the cabinet in which he kept old boxes of things—boxes of memories of the women he'd loved before—and pulled down the brown leather bag that held his shotgun.

The leather had gone stiff and cracked from nonuse. The pieces of the disassembled gun were dry and gritty, too, and the father spent that night in the basement's low light with a can of oil and a white rag and he worked until each moving part had been cleaned and replaced.

The next morning, with the factory under repair and the forecasted rain waiting for afternoon, the father took the brothers to the gun range and taught them how to shoot, the oldest brother taking three shots for each of the youngest's one, the oldest brother concerned with the feel of it, the feel of the warm gray gunmetal against his cheek, the sweet smell of the powder, the force of the recoil, the youngest brother concerned with the speed of the wind, the size of the target to shoot, the distance to the target and the end of the field beyond. The father and the boys noticed the difference: that one should be so quick to draw and the other so loathe.

This was all before the factory strike, before the union meetings in backrooms of bars during which the men made lists of demands and chose leaders, before the company called for wage cuts and the union started handing out strike pay, before negotiations broke and the men circled the plant, threatened anyone who'd cross. The father declined to march himself, his legs still slow. But rather than stay home, he drove a shuttle in the family Plymouth between union headquarters and the factory fence, carried fresh men and signs and sandwiches and beer, always in a short-sleeved shirt that exposed his scars, the jagged too-white patches of fallow skin where hair had been burned off and would never grow again.

The strike lasted through the heat and humidity of the summer, the father sweating thick into the black of the Plymouth's leather. He told none of the men nor the brothers nor the third wife how afraid he was for world's end and how badly he wished for the comfort of his eye goggles and earplugs. How badly he did not want to seem meek.

There wasn't any religion in this fear. The father had never been a religious man. Mornings on the assembly line or at the strike line, he'd stand outside from the circle of those men who were religious, and he'd watch them pray for a safety and a happiness that, as far as he could understand, weren't likely to come and wouldn't be worth much if they ever did. It was just, he thought, the natural order of all things to end: as with the lives of plants and trees and wives so with the lives of the seas and the land, all Earth and the universe. And he couldn't think after the end there would be anything more than blind black space like the space after the edge of a map.

Once the contract was settled and all the men were back to work, the line restarted and the company pushed to cover the shortfall, to rebuild inventory lost in the fire and inventory unassembled during the strike, the line now almost as fast as the day of the fire and almost as wild. The men struggled to make numbers and everyone was still bitter. It wasn't long before rumors of the factory closing began to spread, and the rumors spread almost as fast as fire.

There were layoffs that emptied half the factory—the company started with the newest guys and worked their way up by seniority, stopping just short of the father. Layoffs at other factories in the city followed. Plants closed, companies ended.

And with all these layoffs, there was a time then when, for the brothers, the daytime neighborhood grew full to bursting with fathers. Fathers at baseball games and school plays. Fathers in grocery stores and in line at the bank. Fathers in backyards playing catch or setting tea parties. Fathers fixing parts of houses that didn't need fixing or trying to fix parts that were past repair and couldn't be fixed. Fathers mowing already-mowed lawns, mowing them again and again leaving only small snippets of fresh grass blade tips as seed to plant and grow again, to grow thicker. Fathers played and fixed and mowed because there was nothing else left to do that they knew how to do and none of them believed there was anything new he could learn or that he wanted to learn, nothing more than assembling cars. The only thing more fearsome for fathers than the thought of the chaos of parts, of cars unassembled, was the thought of days spent sitting on couches, hours like parts left unassembled.

For the father and the other long-timers who remained at the factory, though, layoffs meant doing the jobs of two men at once, working two stations at a time, assembling cars with only a skeleton crew. This factory was open but nearly closed, these men the only life in a factory in various stages of death, of death and rebirth or death and undeath. The father believed all along that an end was imminent. And, just as he thought, it wasn't long before the factory closed altogether.

In this time, when their neighborhood friends were taken away by fathers, the brothers saw less of each other. The youngest brother stayed closer and closer to home, stopped exploring the neighborhood and the yard, choosing instead to read and to watch the world through the window. The oldest brother went further and further from home, further away from this woman who was not their mother and this father who was not the same kind of father as others they knew. This oldest brother found friends in faraway neighborhoods near the water or near the rundown places, the dark alleys, of the city.

There was once when the youngest brother and the oldest brother were together alone in the kitchen of the house, together at the table. The youngest brother had cereal because it was morning. The oldest brother had a beef sandwich he'd made for himself. The youngest brother's pale face was lit soft by the glass-covered bulb overhead and the house felt cooler than usual.

The oldest brother asked him, "So, you have a girlfriend yet?"

The youngest brother looked up from his bowl. He said, "I don't know." There were girls at school who he sometimes talked to but couldn't ever think of anything important to say. He would get nervous and feel sick just like he was nervous and felt sick now. "Am I supposed to?"

"No. It's fine," said the oldest brother. "You'll be fine. You'll figure it all out." The oldest brother crumpled the paper towel on which he'd made his sandwich and stood. He stopped for a second like he had something else to say. The youngest brother looked up at him. "No, you'll probably be fine," he said and walked back toward the stairs to their bedroom.

That was all they talked about then and the last time they talked or even saw each other for a week afterward.

Then came the year of fires.

Houses burned in this year and houses were abandoned in this year, houses the factory men could no longer afford and in which they no longer had reason to live. Families moved away. What houses weren't burned for insurance stood empty or were torn down or were burned down too, these not for money but for the hell of it.

Buildings all through the city were burned. Empty houses and shuttered factories and boarded-up stores and bars and historical buildings, historical buildings from the old city that no longer was, buildings preserved for decoration, buildings that were meeting places, libraries and restaurants and speakeasies. Most all of these buildings burned. Those that didn't burn were tagged, sprayed over in long neon marks, some as art, but most as territorial claims or painted threats.

What seemed like every night, their neighborhood would glow red with sparks and then flames that flashed and slashed and died and came undead in embers that popped and cracked until morning. Fall air smelled thin and sweet like burning wood. Breaths turned thick with ash. The youngest brother believed when he coughed he spat the homes of his few friends, that he spat wet woodsmoke.

The other boys in the neighborhood disappeared with the houses, gone to wherever people who move away go. The oldest brother gone to wherever the oldest brother went. Their street grew quieter with new weeds pressing up through the asphalt cracks formed by winter and weeds pressing up into the yards around theirs. Weeds rising as houses came down. Weeds turning to wild weeds and wild grass and wild flowers, all in tall stalks that the wind would blow and bend.

Everything was lonely.

Most days, the youngest brother stayed inside. Though some days he would stand on the porch and watch the wind arc the weeds toward the lake and the river, watch the neighborhood bend toward water, this old neighborhood now going to prairie or rewilded frontier.

The houses around them continued to fall until theirs was the only house left standing on the block, the only house left in the neighborhood that hadn't been burned down or torn down or abandoned to nature, and at night after the city lights faded and the cars stopped rolling past, the animals took over. The backyard was all jungle whispers and whines with the occasional screaming call.

The youngest brother lay alone these nights in the brothers' shared room with the window open, waiting for the oldest brother and listening to the world outside. He'd loved to explore their yard when the neighborhood wasn't wild. Now he wondered with this wild whether he'd ever have the courage to explore unfound spaces again, whether he'd ever be the first to see anything. And these nights he'd lay awake in his bed in the quiet of the house and listen for sounds and he'd call out to no one the names of the animals, one for each letter of the alphabet, each in the order of the alphabet—right or wrong, animals he hoped were there, wildlife he wished to find around them, dreamed to find around them. And when for a letter he couldn't think of any animals he knew, of real animals, he imagined and named new animals, imaginary beings whose sounds grew from the weeds and wind and burnt timber and fallen steel of their city forest.

Nights when the oldest brother stayed gone, the youngest brother worried. Some of these nights it rained and there was thunder and lightning and the radio news talked of floods, of low-lying roads washed out or interstate underpasses under water, of the river rising. When cold came, some of these nights it snowed and the first snow stuck high in the trees and the further snow fell further to branches, to bushes, and to the foundations of former homes. Snow stuck to bent reeds and flowers. Snow fell to the ground, covered their lawn in white, covered the forest floor. And these nights the youngest brother wondered whether the oldest brother had meant to come home but had somehow gotten lost, lost his tracks, like the oldest brother was a fairy tale Hansel, alone and afraid and crumb-less. The youngest brother feared he'd failed his brother somehow, left him lost, let him go.

The father's fears were different. The factory and the forest. Their neighborhood embers. The absence of the oldest. The floods. All of it, the father feared, was his fault, all of it the result of this evil he believed he possessed, and, if not evil, this bad whatever-it-was. The eye goggles and the earplugs no longer helped. Even in their smooth, safe remove from the world around him, the father decided, he still hurt all he loved, whether in pregnant birthdeath or in starvation and abandonment. It was the world that needed earplugs and eye goggles, he believed, to protect against him. To him, the close of the factory was another sort of legend, the last lines of life's atlas: give of yourself before all else is taken.

He didn't sell or burn the house. He didn't leave. He gave himself.

First, he took a day off from work and drove the brothers and the third wife to the river. They parked the car and they boarded a steamer ship that steamed them out to an island in the strait, to the amusement park. And that afternoon they acted as a family. The father bought ride tickets and funnel cakes. They visited the zoo and took a gondola to the top of the Ferris wheel. They rode the Wild Mouse, the Sky Streak, the Nightmare, the Screamer, and the Falling Star. The park had a railroad that ran along the water, and they watched the boats on the river and the falling city across it. The father bought souvenirs for the brothers. He took a strip of photo booth pictures of himself for the third wife.

And late that night the father went to the basement.

This night in the basement there was just the quiet of the lone light bulb hanging from the ceiling. The father with his scarred arms out in front of him, his legs tucked under. His eyes covered. His ears plugged. There was the crack of a shotgun flame no taller than the lighter that no longer lit the cigarettes he would not smoke. There was the impression of the goggles' strap inverted.

The third wife was asleep.

The oldest brother was away.

The youngest brother had reached the end of the alphabet. He named the sound "zombie."

## Part II

The oldest brother worked in the prison kitchen and in the late morning among the steel, he poured the contents of industrial-sized cans into pots of boiling water that he stirred slowly with a strainer until the peas or the carrots or the beans or the whatever cooked through.

He wore an apron and a hairnet and latex gloves that struggled to fit the full bulk of his hands and clenched at his wrists. He carried steam trays to the line, and on the line he spooned vegetables or beans or rice onto plates he passed under glass to the incarcerated others. He knew not to smile.

This was his every day, and, as much as he hated it, he knew the father would've been proud of him working each day on a line. One man among many. One purpose among many. For the oldest brother, there was something about the closing of the factory that had broken him of the need to work, the satisfaction of it, and turned him toward stealing instead. Everything belongs to everybody, he believed, and you have to take what's yours before you're left with nothing.

Although, midway through his sentence—maybe out of boredom, maybe out of imagination—he began to experiment with recipes. One day, he added thyme to the peas. Instead of the usual gray, they tasted bright. Another day, he diced an onion into the pintos, and—more than just mush—they tasted crisp and new. Another day, he boiled the potatoes before he fried them and the next day after that he boiled them even longer, boiled them until they flaked, and then dried them in the oven and dropped them one piece by one piece into the fryer. And then as he pulled the potatoes up out of the oil, he salted them. One day, he snuck a can of chili powder to his station and he used it to spice the fries. At the line, the other men smiled for once. The lunchroom ate loud. Some men came back for seconds.

The morning of his last day inside, he persuaded the head chef to allow him a gross of eggs and some produce, to let him set up a station at the end of the lunch line. His station was a low table and he had to bend his broad shoulders to huddle over it. But he worked the hot plate two pans at a time, four eggs per man, and he made omelettes to order. Hungry and mean as they were, he worked each pan until it was fully cooked, until whatever germs might attach had burnt off. And with each egg he passed under the glass, he said, "Here you are sir. Please enjoy." The last man through the line, one of his fellow cooks from kitchen duty, said, "You're a good one. A good man. I'd follow you anywhere." The oldest brother didn't say anything. He just looked the man in the eyes and smiled.

//////////////

It started in basements, some combination of loneliness and drug-resistant mold, living spores below the surface that grew from what, no one knew for sure, and became airborne in the wet must of the Indiana underground. Most imagined it had moved core to crust, that it was forged in the core's kiln, cooled in the mantle, and finished in the condensation pooled by molten rock rising. They saw it stalagmitic, soaking up from the Earth, surfacing through foundry, breaching steel and wires and walls.

Others were certain there was nothing earthly about it. Some asteroid spotted with alien molecules, they said, that survived the burn of the atmosphere as the rock broke and became meteoroid and meteorite, these molecules reacting with the gases of life and death at the Earth's surface and all of it converting molecules to stalactitic spores that vaporized maybe or liquefied and seeped into the grass, the dirt, the groundwater, and into homes. Some even claimed to have seen the shoot of the star as it crossed over and fell. That they wished on it.

First it was shut-ins and doomsayers outside Muncie. They'd go down to their basements to check supplies for the end of the world, spend days counting cans, scheduling out the water supply, all the while inhaling apocalypse, unknowingly. Then there were the invalids, the lesser-abled, who had no choice but to spend most of their time in their homes. And then the recluses, the men, mostly, middle-aged, who'd moved back in with their parents after how many years of trying to make a career in hard times, a career out of nothing. And then the teenagers got it. Not the popular kids, but the outcasts, the ones who'd spend Friday nights at home alone in the glow of electronic screens, in the company of Internet friends.

What they learned later: The spores absorb through the skin or the eyes or nose or mouth and combine with certain fluids in the body. Together they eat away at the parts of the brain responsible for empathy and love. Without these parts, the social brain shuts down and the eyes glaze over. The breath sickens. Capillaries start to retain carbon and the carbon and the mold and the oxygen compound in the blood to produce a sort of acid that petrifies the organs. A human rust. The muscles still work, though the joints embrittle. The heart and the brain survive, are held in suspension, encased in a fat-like gel. But the rest of the body drains pigment and moisture and turns crisp, like it's been fried white. The body moves forward on its own, continues to move, eyes blank, arms out. All of it, all of them, always seemingly searching.

The spores spread slowly, in fits and starts. It was weeks before anyone even thought to be wary of the pale. They didn't fully understand the biology of it at the time, and, probably because of what they'd seen in movies, they assumed the virus was easily communicated, transmitted through teeth or blood or through air or water or proximity. The news warned people to stay inside, to protect themselves from the imminent outbreak. This only hastened the spread in Muncie and the virus ate away at others in the town, ate through most of the town. Without logic, more cases were reported in other isolated towns—on an outlying island of Japan and in Siberia and at the international base in Antarctica—and all of the governments involved initiated quarantine, terrified that, in the unusually hot summer, the epidemic might go pandemic.

In Indiana, they drew a ring around the town and cut it off from the world, built borders and closed them, called it a "no-go" zone, even though not everyone was infected. Still, without understanding the cause, they told everyone in the quarantine to keep to themselves. Blared these instructions over loudspeakers suspended high on tall poles erected outside the border fence. Told them to stay inside unless absolutely necessary, to live in basements. And in a short time, the many who weren't infected became the few who weren't infected became the nobody.

Maybe it was a symptom of the virus or maybe it was some last thing still human, some last reflex toward life, but after a week the people of the town began to emerge from their homes, these people now zombies, these people now looking for something.

They formed no hordes, the virus refusing the urge to congregate. Instead they walked as individuals. They slowly roamed. They poked through the quiet remains of the town. They went looking for a boundary, for a border, and they stood there at the fenceline, stabbed crisp white remains of fingers and toes at the high concrete barriers, tapped at the glass windows embedded in the walls for observation. To those on the other side, these stabs were silent, though, absorbed in the thick of the panes, these panes made to block bullets, to keep the undead inside.

*⁄⁄⁄⁄⁄⁄⁄⁄⁄⁄⁄⁄⁄⁄⁄⁄*

The oldest brother sat in the far corner of a double-wide, this trailer in the floodlit raindark not much different from the trailer in which he signed up for the Guard, and that trailer not much different from the trailer at the gate-edge of the prison, the trailer where they passed back his shirt and his pants and his wallet and his hat, the same trailer where they'd taken those things to begin with a year earlier. This was a thing he'd gotten used to, this passing back and forth, having things and then not and then having them again and then handing them over again. The most recent time before this, it was in exchange for a Guard uniform. He still wasn't quite sure why he'd signed the enlistment papers. It wasn't any sense of duty, he didn't think. Maybe he was thinking of the late father, of pleasing his memory, making his corpse father proud, that maybe there was something about pride that it could resurrect the dead. Maybe he thought it would be brave to protect the world from the virus, from the zombies. Maybe he thought he was still serving a sentence, that jail wasn't punishment enough for having left the youngest brother alone all those nights, the brother who was like him in so many more ways than not.

Whatever it was, he could hear the shouting of the protestors at the fenceline a half mile away—families and friends of those trapped inside and others who just wanted to be there, just wanted to shout for reasons the oldest brother didn't think could ever matter—and even with his minimal training he knew it was his job to use whatever force it might take to quiet them.

Across the trailer, the commander of the unit entered and the oldest brother and the six other boys, none of them brothers for real but brothers for now, stood and saluted. The commander said, "Brothers, be smart out there."

All the boys said, "Yes sir," with the tallest boy saying it loudest. Or at least his voice was lowest and sharpest. The tallest boy had thick and dark brown hair and an accent from the west. In formations and in drills, the boys always lined up this way: in order of height, from tallest to shortest, and here in a semicircle inside the double-wide, the oldest brother noticed for maybe the first time that their other features descended too. That the voice of the next tallest boy was a note less low, a note less sharp, his accent from a place less west, more mountainous. His hair was somewhat thinner. And same for the next boy and the next. The shortest had the least brown hair, the thinnest hair. His voice was high and flat, his words formed in the tones of the east. The oldest brother stood in the middle, an octave below and an octave above the ends of the line. As the commander reiterated the plan of attack, the oldest brother thought about the youngest brother and how impossible it was that he would ever fit in this line. He thought also about how some things can be impossible one day and possible the next. How it seemed like, with everything becoming something else, there wasn't really anything now that couldn't change so entirely.

"Boys, be bold. Be brave. Be safe. Fight well. You are dismissed," said the commander. He clicked his heels together and exited the trailer. The Guard boys followed him, filed toward the trailer door, grabbed their muck jackets and boots from the rack near the door, and stepped out into the cold of the rain.

In the night with the rain and the lightning in flashes and the high lofted light balloons softly flooding the long stretches of farm land with soft light, the light refracting in rain drops, droplets like prisms or crystals, these crystals seeming to float in the air, one replaced immediately by the next, the air seeming still in this way in all of this tumult, the air a waiting army of light—in all of this, the Guard boys marched across the farmland. The land was wet grass and mud. The mud clung to their boots on the rise and fell with the rain before each down step only to rise again.

After the farm there was the road to the city. The oldest brother took the center of the road and led the Guard boys along the road's yellow divider. They marched toward the walled-off city in the distance and the ring of protestors that stood before it, outside it. The rain had wetted his face and his legs were thick and heavy with the wet and the mud and the hill they had to cross. But still he could see it rising from the valley, the lit-up outside with the concrete barriers and barbed wire and the news vans and trailers and tents and the other Guard units behind cover and the signs—government-issued warnings and homemade protests—and the masses of people watching and chanting and throwing rocks and bottles. And just beyond: the pitch black of the quarantine.

The people had been out there for eighty days, some of them longer. First were the families and friends of the ones infected and also the ones not infected but trapped. They looked for their people through the glass, crowded around the small windows, set up cameras and video feeds. If they saw one, they'd shout, and the shouts would raise anyone on this side of the barrier who'd given up for the day or fallen asleep, and they'd all crowd to the windows again. The ones inside could never hear the shouts; the walls were too thick and too high and the wind too downcast and there were the sounds of the trucks setting up more barriers, barriers beyond barriers, and more barriers beyond those. An airtight quarantine, they called it. After a week of sleepless nights, looking pale and red-eyed and zombic themselves, the families and friends got frustrated and angry. The Guard troops moved them back from the windows, set up new windows to watch the old windows, these families and friends now two thick panes from the inside.

Which is when the others came. The curious and the paranoid and the scared and the furious. They came in campers and buses, parked them along the outside of the last barrier, built a barrier of their own, and began shouting on their own. They shouted for the rights of the people inside, the infected and the not, all of them. They were joined by the families and the friends and the news media, who aired stories about government restrictions and special orders and secrecy. They called the quarantine "internment," said "not again" with all they had in their hands: cameras, bullhorns, signs, foundry, and, later, guns.

Each of the Guard boys carried a device that screened pictures of their targets, the nine worst agitators—the commander had called them professional miscreants—who every morning would whip up the crowd into a frenzy and who weren't afraid to use violence or to inspire others to use violence to fend off the Guard. To capture and remove the agitators: this was their mission.

The agitators weren't given names, but looking at his screen a ninth time, the oldest brother was sure he recognized at least a couple of the faces as boys from back home in Detroit. One scarred round face he was sure he'd seen in prison. All of the faces were young—some tattooed or misshaped and angry—but they were still fresh somehow. And yet, only as the Guard boys drew closer to the mass of protestors did they realize that many of the protestors were wearing bandanas or hoods over their heads and faces, that many left only their eyes exposed.

"No way we'll be able to tell them apart," said the shortest. His flat voice blended into the whining neigh of the cavalry horses and revolving tank tracks in the front-line formation of the Guard around them. It was just loud enough for the Guard boys to hear him and they all agreed.

"Guess we'll just have to take them all in," said the second tallest. The oldest brother laughed and the others laughed with him.

"Look at their eyes," the oldest brother said. "We'll be able to identify them by their eyes. We'll wait until dusk. Memorize their eyes. Then we move while the peaceful ones sleep. Night's when the worst people work."

The rain stopped with daylight and the cold of the wet dawn gave way to the wet warmth of day. The sun broke through mid-morning and baked the small lakes and rivers of mud of the farmland, these small bodies of wet dirt shrinking away muddy moisture and the moisture leaving tracks of evaporated mud on the boy's uniforms, on their pant legs and coat arms and lapels. They sweated in the sun and the sweat mixed with the air's dirt in a paste that coated their foreheads and eyelids and lips and stuck in the short wisps of hair of their unshaven faces.

The ground was earth and the air was earth and the boys were earth and there was a moment then when the oldest brother, seated at the head of an unfolded card table at the rear of the Guard encampment, suddenly felt as though they'd all been buried alive. For this moment he felt each blink turn his eyes to mud and each breath coat the insides of him, his organs. Seeing and breathing were a struggle and the oldest brother felt suffocated with death. Like we, too, are zombies of Muncie, he thought. And for this moment he understood the scratching at the barricade windows, the scratching for life, and he understood the cries of the families and friends and the wind-winged shouts of the agitators. There was discomfort in this, the oldest brother thought, to feel so close to those he was supposed to fight. And he shifted his weight in his seat, tried to push the thought away. It was his way of making the moment pass quickly.

The shortest boy called for a game of euchre and the oldest brother said "yes" and another of the boys pulled a deck of cards from the inside pocket of his muck coat. Euchre was the oldest brother's game—the game he'd play with the youngest brother and the father on trips up north during summers and sometimes winters when the father was still alive. One cold afternoon game, the father allowed him his first taste of whiskey.

"Deal goes to the first black jack," said the oldest brother as he passed cards around the table to the three shortest Guard boys.

"Dollar a trick?" the shortest boy asked.

"Make it two," said another.

After the deal, the oldest brother called for spades as the trump and opened with the king of that suit. His partner across the table, the shortest boy, laid down the ace, took the first trick, and opened the next trick with the queen of diamonds.

The next boy laid down the ace of diamonds. He said to the oldest brother, "Come on, show us your diamonds. I know you've got some. I can see them reflecting in your eyes."

"Sorry, boy. No diamonds," the oldest brother said. And instead, he laid down the jack of spades, the trump card, and won the trick.

"Goddammit," said one of the other boys. He tried to push his chair back but it stuck in the mud, the feet of it burrowed. There was the wet smell of mud and heat.

During all of this, the three taller boys who'd chosen not to play stood watch, blocking the sun and making it seem as though the shorter boys were playing cards in the dark, as though they were playing in a basement. And past the trailers and the trucks and the tanks there was shouting, which, to the oldest brother, sounded like fall wind outside, words like brown leaves blown and muffled by closed windows. Like maybe this wasn't war at all, but a Halloween party at a friend's house like they used to have and the boys were all in costume waiting around for a meal someone's mother thought would be clever—spaghetti brains and cooked carrot fingers and meatball eyes. Again, he shifted in his seat.

For the last trick of the hand, the last trick to win the hand, the one boy led with the last of the aces, the ace of clubs, and the shortest boy laid down his last low club, as well. The other boy had a club-suited queen left. They all turned to the oldest brother, who held his last card against his chest for a moment. He smiled as they waited. There was something satisfying in it, in making them wait. Holding the jack of clubs, the bower. That there was a card that could change suits, a club that in this game, for this round, could become the second-high spade, that there was this card that could be more powerful than an ace if played right. And he played it and laughed and he and the shortest boy took the hand.

The sun rose over the shoulders of the standing boys, growing hotter with each trick of the first two hands. After the third hand, the tallest boy got the other standing boys to follow him to the mess tent. The sun went with them, barricaded by a thick patch of rolling clouds graying in from the west.

The sitting boys finished out the round, continued the game in this cloud-covered near-dark. The shortest boy went it alone twice and won both times. One time, the oldest brother trumped the one boy's trump card and the one boy slammed his fist on the unsteady table. As a team, the shortest boy and the oldest brother only gave away five points before hitting their ten and collecting the money. The other two boys stood up from the table as soon as the last card went down.

"You boys don't want to play another round?" asked the shortest boy smiling, his laugh flat and high.

The one boy said, "It's a cold weather game. Only fun when you don't have anything else to do and your toes are frozen."

"Yeah," said the other boy. "Maybe if we were ice fishing."

"We sure as hell are not ice fishing," said the tallest boy, just back from the mess tent with the other Guard boys. "But we've got some fish to catch."

The protestors were loudest at the front lines. There was a writhing horde of them near the one gate into the quarantine. The sound was its own gate between the Guard boys and Muncie, between the Guard boys and the zombie town. There was a line of boys from other Guard units at the front, all of them suited in bulletproof ceramic and holding up shields like ancient fighters. Behind the boys dug in at the front, there was a Guard unit from Minnesota standing in the beds of trucks working water cannons. Whenever a protestor looked like he might advance—the

Guard boys called it "going hostile" or "going red"—the Minnesota boys would direct two dozen gallons at his chest to knock him down. Most would fall backward, some at an angle, and the Guard and the protestors would go back to their separate untouching distances.

From the front along the valley's descent, the oldest brother and the other Guard boys could see the heights of the quarantine. It was dusk and the quarantine was nearing dark again and eerie. There was an eclipse of moths hovering. All the oldest brother knew about moths was that they're like butterflies without color and that they eat holes in things, sweaters and linen. Their basement at home smelled like mothballs and gunpowder.

The Guard boys took up an offensive position and winged themselves into a V, with the oldest brother at the blade edge.

"We go on orders," said the shortest boy.

"We don't shoot unless shot at," said the tallest boy.

The oldest brother said, "Look out for each other. Stay in formation."

In the spray of the water cannon and the salt steam of the tear gas, the protestors looked like an ocean's waves, these guard boys a skiff, and the oldest brother tried to remember a prayer for sailors and safety at sea from the couple of times he'd paid attention to services in jail. He thought he'd landed on a hymn, but realized after a moment it was just a song about a wreck, about the Edmund Fitzgerald, the freighter that sank in Lake Superior. They played it at the father's funeral. It was one of the father's favorites. That anyone could think they were big enough to survive a lake called Superior.

Lake or ocean, this body of water was in angry motion now as the Guard boys undocked toward it, afloat in their helmets and masks, into the dark of the wet valley. The rain came again suddenly and in a wash.

The Guard boys angled through the protestors, first scanning each one's eyes for an agitator and then pressing the crowd away with riot shields. One of the protestors pressed back and the shortest boy raised his baton and struck the kid where neck met head. The kid fell. An older woman lay limp on the ground to impede the Guard boys and the tallest boy kicked at her ribs, flattening her into a heap they all could step over. One kid tossed a stone that simply tapped against one Guard boy's vest. Another sent a bigger stone toward the oldest brother who saw it coming and deflected it with his shield. There was a crash of glass behind them and another crash in front of them and to each of their sides, this glass dropping like rain under the lightning and thunder of the storm.

Their V detached at the tip into slashes and collapsed into hyphens and came apart further into a sort of code, long short long, the oldest brother alone in the middle and surrounded. Inside this helmet and behind these goggles, all of the eyes began to look the same—grainy, flat, and mad. He thought he saw an agitator, one of the ones he had thought earlier he might recognize, and he took a hand off his shield and reached for the kid's mask and pulled it down. It was just a kid like any other, not one of the ones they'd targeted, but the kid's eyes turned wild and the kid reached across at the oldest brother's shield and tore it to the ground. The oldest brother raised his elbow at the kid and knocked him to the ground next to the shield. The oldest brother went to recover the shield but the protestors filled in around him and the kid, the crowd drowning them both, and so instead the oldest brother thrashed upward and raised his weapon.

"Don't make me take you," he shouted. He wasn't sure anyone could hear. Though the crowd around him parted and he could see again the tallest boy, his own weapon raised, his elbows striking temples of the protestors around him.

The oldest brother tried to regain direction. Rising on the hill to his right was the water cannon. He could feel its spray, this spray now constant, this entire crowd sea now "going red." The other Guard boys had disappeared, as well, and he could not see the barrier to the quarantine.

He looked forward deeper into the crowd. At an edge where all things seemed to come together, he caught a gray glint of darkening cloudlight off the gunmetal of a muzzle. He yelled the word "Gun." The tallest boy heard the shout and pulled out his own gun. And then all at once all of the gray seemed to be gun.

The oldest brother raised his gray gun and shot toward the glint or where the glint had been. The gun whipcracked and flashed flame. The crowd crashed and rolled in screaming waves. The oldest brother shot again and the tallest boy shot too and there was the shortest boy standing again and he shot too.

There were shots that came back, that were returned. The oldest brother could hear their whizz even in the dim of his helmet. There was one shot that knocked his helmet off into the mud. The oldest brother fired two more shots before he saw another shot aimed at him, at the open of his mouth where lips meet teeth.

He stood there stunned for a second.

He wondered where the bullet had gone.

He fell to the water, to the mud, the ground.

*////////////////*

It ended in culs-de-sac, at fence-ends of city parks, at the shore of the Prairie Creek Reservoir. It ended in spaces where things end, where they can't go further. After the battle at the barricades and the removal of the agitators, the decision was made to close the quarantine, to retake the town for the fully living. The Guard boys, or what was left of them, rode by ranks into the city, some in full hazmat, others in their muck coats and boots with hoods and masks and goggles and gloves. They swept through Muncie like drawing a maze. Clear an outer arc, lay a new barricade, cut back toward the start, lay a new barricade, clear another arc, an inner arc, a new barricade, a cut-back, a barricade. They had rejected a plan simply to burn the city, and instead burned trails with the slow frictional draw of their boots along city ground. Guard boys like regiment guards of a labyrinth. Water cannons like staffs. Herding zombies toward these city ends.

They went house to house. Gathered zombies from their homes. Cleared structures from bottom to top and top to bottom. Dug into gutters and basements. Parachuted onto roofs. Hung off eaves and vaulted through windows. They found cars undriven, beds unslept upon, broken picture frames and empty bottles, baby blankets unswaddling, messages unanswered. They found animals half-eaten, torsos intact, heads dislodged. They found the few frightened survivors huddling in closets and other dark, secure spaces.

The Guard boys swept the zombies toward the train station and loaded them two by two into the boxcars of an empty freight. There was a midnight screel as the train wheels started to turn, as the train moved out from Muncie, and then a whistle and then the steam from the coal car, steam that funneled like a smokestack up toward the gray of dark clouds where it dispersed or disappeared or simply stopped. The steam of the train's engine drew a path to the facility in California, a three-story shale-green prison built in the nothing center of the deep desert, in this other valley, Death Valley.

Soon, after the end of the nine months, the news vans moved on and the Guard boys moved on. They were needed elsewhere. The other outbreaks followed the Guard's Muncie plan and cleared their own quarantines, fortified their own facilities.

There was a short investigation and the underground was declared safe. Oil rigs went back into production. Cities made new tunnels. Farmers planted new fence posts and crops. Dogs buried bones. Children started digging again, digging holes in backyards, holes through the earth in hopes of one day reaching China. The more imaginative thought they might loop a long thread through such a hole, grab hold of the Earth, fling us all toward the moon, the sun, and beyond into the far depths of outer space.

In Detroit, in the downtown, near the river, with the wind-blown reeds bent toward water, they dedicated a memorial to the zombie war. They built it in the center of a park. There was a small round fountain that spilled out from the topsides into a shallow pool with, at its center, an eternal flame kept lit by pipefulls of gas pumped from a tank underground. Around the fountain there was a long, low wall of marble into which they etched dozens of young faces—the faces of the hometown Guard boys who were lost, the oldest brother among them. The etchings weren't deep, the relief easier felt with the tips of fingers than seen. But in the small light of the flame and the late light of evening, the etchings would throw short shadows, the faces low-lit, pipe-fed, pale, and undead.

## Part III

The youngest brother found his father head-cracked and backwards on the yellowing gray of the morning's basement floor. He screamed the father's name and knelt at his side. He kneeled over the father and pressed the palms of his fists into the valley between the father's ribs and stomach. He pressed nine times, once for every full year they'd felt like a real family. He kissed what was left of the father's mouth, breathed air into the father's lungs and with each breath could feel the father's lungs expand and after each breath could feel the contraction in thin haloes of air escaping. He thought this air had to be the air of death, that the smell of this air must be the smell of death, the foul taste of it. But deeper inside him it did not feel bad; it felt like love exhaled. And the youngest brother tried to swallow all of it he could, to let the wet of it soak into his own lungs and into his blood. Still, the father lay shot open and lifeless on the floor.

There was no grand, elegiac funeral, just a moment in the outer parlor of the morgue, the third wife in black veil and tears and the oldest brother, his hair fully grown, in the farthest corner twisting a cigarette—the father's brand—around and between his left-hand knuckles. The youngest brother wore a suit. Whatever prayers the three said were silent and their own. These prayers now pleas.

And then at the cemetery, they lowered the boxed body of the father by pulleys into a dirt pit. This pit now a grave. This modest stone now a marker.

In the cemetery, there were trees like they had at home—maples whose winged helicopter seedlings had spun circles to the ground. When they were younger, the oldest brother and the youngest brother would pick the fresh dropped seeds from the grass of their backyard, split open the pods, and stick the seeds, wings intact, to the bridges of their noses. They spent afternoons running through the yard like this, like they were rhinoceroses or the world's only two unicorns and they ran into the house and into the kitchen where the third wife would stop them and say, "Don't be ridiculous." If he was home, the father would say, "Leave them be. They're just doing what boys do. They're just being brothers."

But to the youngest brother, the death of the father seemed it might sever whatever bond there was between the brothers. The two of them, he decided, had only ever been linked by the father. And while maybe they both grew from that same source of seed, there was more to everything that grows than just seed, wasn't there? There are maples spread all over; that they're all maples doesn't mean they're the same, that they grow the same branches, the same leaves. It doesn't mean they owe each other anything. Like love. It's more important that they're trees and alive. Everything grows from the earth and gets returned to the earth and new things grow from the same earth. Everything grows from everything and any claim he might have to being a brother might just as easily make him brother to every boy that's ever been—alive, dead, or otherwise.

And in the next months, the oldest brother and the youngest brother saw each other less and less, the oldest brother staying further and further away. In this time, there was just the quiet of the house, of the neighborhood, the city. In this quiet the youngest brother could feel silent brushes of chill wind like the body of the father, watching. The phantasmic cold quiet of the night house. It was unsettling.

The youngest brother tried to resist the quiet. He scavenged parts and he built a transistor radio and nights alone at home he would scan the dial listening for voices of the living and the lonely. He lay in bed with the radio held close to his ear in hopes of hearing something more than the cracks and crackles and sand sounds of the radio static, in hopes of hearing something he would not mistake for a backyard animal, for the backyard animals he'd already heard before and named.

Most nights there was nothing except static. But some nights—maybe by tricks of his brain, maybe by tricks of physics or space-time—he thought he heard the almost indistinct voice of a woman reading numbers. He swiveled in his chair, tucked his feet under the desk they shared, centered himself on the radio. The numbers seemed random: 22, 9, 47, 4,000, 12, and so on. Dimensions maybe, lengths widths and heights, or times or coordinates, plot points to a place. The voice was soft and blanketing and warm. He refused what he wanted to think—it was the voice of his mother. He forced himself to believe the more likely thing, that this was the voice of a stranger, a woman who'd been lost a long time and who'd been desperate to be found. He imagined her alone on a desert island. The pilot of an old plane that crash-landed. His own alive Earhart. Her palm trees to his maple. He in the dark and the cold and she in the sun and the hot. The two of them connected at the arc and crash of transistor waves.

Some nights he would try to answer. He'd say hello and call out his name and his location. He'd read numbers of his own, latitudes and longitudes and birthdates and acreages, floor plans and beam-widths. But the voice only lasted so long before the Earth would turn and the numbers would fade and anyway there was no way, he thought, his numbers would ever reach her or make the least sense or mean anything to her if they did make sense. The stranded can only dream of being un-stranded, he thought, just like the dead can only dream of being undead. Even so, the youngest brother made notes of the numbers, the numbers of the voice and his own numbers. And for fun, he invented equations to try to calculate the numbers into something meaningful and, when the equations made no meaning, instead he drew crude plans for buildings using these numbers.

Once, after dark, the oldest brother invited the youngest brother out with his friends. They drove in the family Plymouth to parts of the city the youngest brother had never been, south past the bridge and the fort, down near the salt mine. The oldest brother's friends all wore dark clothes and zip-up hoodies and they smoked cigarettes. They turned away from the streetlights and the mine's front gate onto an unpaved side street next to a chain link fence. "There's our hole," said the old-est brother between drags, and the boys took turns crawling under a pulled-up tangle of steel.

They gathered on the other side and walked out together into the salt yard. There was salt everywhere. White hills and mountains of it. The oldest brother and his friends climbed the mounds and from the tops of the salt mounds they called down to the youngest brother to climb up too and he did. He wedged his fingers as dry anchors in salt, the rock salt scraping and scratching his fingers, his fingers stung by the salt as he climbed. At the top, he could see the few dim lights of the city and the light off the river and the plumes of the late night factory smokestacks. He looked down and he swayed and he held up his arms to balance. He licked at his palms. He tasted blood and salt, like the last of the broken mouth and breath of the father.

The oldest brother watched the stars. Some were shooting.

Later that night in one of the last neighborhoods, the oldest brother and his friends had the youngest brother wedge his thin fingers into mailboxes and mail slots to pull out envelopes, which they collected in a bag. At the dead end of a street, the boys stood in a circle around the oldest brother as he tore open envelopes one at a time looking for money or information or who knows what else. When no one could see, the youngest brother cried.

This night was the last of the brothers' time together. They had always seemed, at least since that ninth year, to be in a constant state of growing apart. But this was the last they chose to see of each other outside of glancing looks across the driveway or the living room or in the morning hallway, the youngest brother leaving out for school, the oldest brother coming in for sleep. All that was left close of the two of them were their clothes in the one closet across from the bedroom window, this closet that held the oldest brother's night hoodies and faded-sole shoes next to the youngest brother's shirts and pants and a black suit he called his death suit.

The next time the youngest brother used the suit was the first day of college and the next time after that, four years later, was at the oldest brother's trial. By the time the war started, the oldest brother was halfway through his sentence, and the week he was back they spent at opposite ends of the couch, the third wife between them, watching the news. Then the oldest brother was gone again for a different kind of service.

For the youngest brother, the war meant job interviews and a first day of work, the youngest brother now an assistant to architects, the keeper of plans for a firm outside the city, this firm that built strip malls with anchor stores and filler stores. Every mall plan was a form and every form had a formula, every formula an equation, all of which, the youngest brother found, felt right. In this office, the youngest brother kept blueprints for one-anchor forms and two-anchor forms, upscale forms and downscale forms, symmetrical forms and forms that tapered off or trailed off or would fall off in size into the low shape of the suburban landscape, foot-height by foot-height.

He wasn't there long before the Guard commander's visit telling of the death of the oldest brother.

It was night. There was rain like there always is, thunder like there always is. The Guard commander starched in his dress uniform. The third wife crying before he could get the words out, before he could even clear his throat.

The youngest brother stood behind her in the hallway, already in his death suit. He didn't cry. He just watched the third wife. And in that moment, everything about her seemed suddenly foreign, sharp and unknown, like he'd been snapped out of a trance or snapped into a trance and had suddenly ceased to recognize any piece of her, any strand of her bleached hair, any thread of the dress she wore, her scent, the shape of the flung heap of her heaving body.

The house seemed foreign too. The light was strange and the walls were strange. The linoleum tile floor convexed and concaved under his feet such that he had to shift his weight from foot to foot, like on a boat, like in this house now there was a sea.

The Guard commander left and the third wife went to her bedroom and the youngest brother went outside and sat in the cradle of the roots of the maple among the weeds of the unmowed grass of the backyard. He felt at the roots with his fingertips. He felt the wet grass. He pulled weeds and set them on his lap. The dirt was mud and the rain washed the mud over his suit pants, soaked the mud into the wool of them, buried them.

Everything then seemed to the youngest brother not dead but also not alive. The dead-but-not-dead heap of the third wife, the dead-but-not-dead sea of the quiet house, the dead-but-not-dead eyes of the Guard commander. It couldn't have been the shock of the loss of the oldest brother that colored his world this shade, he thought. He'd always just assumed the oldest brother would die, that his death would be gruesome, that there would be such a visit in the night. It was something else.

He thought then maybe there were things he hadn't realized about seeds and blood. Like maybe blood family is a force that attaches us to the Earth like gravity, or to the world of the living. Like maybe living is a dimension of its own, no more complex than length or width or time. Like maybe blood family is a measurement of living no different than altitude and height. This blood family a plane now disappeared from radar, this youngest brother no longer tracked or trackable, no longer measured. And this was a thought that repeated: that the youngest brother could no longer be measured by the living or, at the very least, that he could no longer measure the living world.

The youngest brother returned to the house's inside. He opened the door to the basement, felt the cold air escape. On a shelf there was the box of the father's things. The box was small. There were so few things he had inherited from the father—the third wife as mother, the oldest brother as absence, the idea of work as salvation, and here, in this box, the earplugs and the blood-stained goggles. And the youngest brother inserted the plugs in his ears and he tied the shot-broken strap of the goggles behind his head and for maybe the first time he heard and he saw as the father for so long had.

In the morning the city felt different as he drove out from it along the interstate. There was a softness to the near-flat skyline in his rearview. The city behind him like old wreckage, some bad, faded memory of a crash not yet cleared, a fire no longer flaming but still alive in some soft way, smoldering maybe, between extinguished and not. That some great danger was passed but its wake not yet unfelt.

The office park seemed different as well. Its long lush streets seemed to bow around the youngest brother as he drove, and the low, sharp lines of the architects' asymmetric building seemed to round and flatten. He could not hear the construction site one lot over, the jackhammers, the Mack trucks and scoop loaders and backhoes and their backup warnings. The youngest brother in his death suit only saw the receptionist at the side of one eye, his boss at the side of the other eye, and the geodesic pattern of the office carpet.

On his ovoid desk were his keyboard and his ovoid screen and his pad and pen and his cup, this cup with a black line drawing of a steamship, this last cup the father ever bought, that the father bought for him. Each morning he would fill the cup with coffee from the dim office kitchen, and this morning the coffee fogged the goggles and he let the steam condense and vaporize, let his workspace disappear and reveal itself again to him in phase change.

There was the dim fluorescence of his space and the dull bustle of the office behind him, the architects and their assistants, the receptionist and the boss. There were doors and windows and cubicles and tall gray stacks of paper and blueprint. And with these goggles and plugs he could focus on his work and turn from his desk only when he chose to, only when he was ready.

This became his every day. The cradle of the streets, the silent construction, and the bowed building. The half-receptionist and the half-boss. The cup. The steam and the unsteam. These moments that separated from one another, split off like atoms or splintered like wood. He could live each moment in its own time, and he held the in-between times as his own.

If there was any ridicule among the architects in the office—of this youngest brother and his goggles and his plugs—he didn't see or hear it. Nearly all of them wear glasses, he thought. They would understand these goggles, this unexplainable instinct to have the world shaped before it's seen.

Even so, there was the one day when the boss came to the youngest brother's office. He went to sit on the edge of the youngest brother's desk but stood instead and said only, "It would just be best if you would remove the goggles and the earplugs whenever there's a client around."

The youngest brother heard only the sharpest angles of this and it took him a moment to process the sounds into words and the words into meaning and the meaning into instructions. The instructions, he thought, were reasonable, though he never met with clients and most days rarely left his desk for long.

At the edge of the desk, he had an inbox that the architects filled with orders, requests for forms for strip malls. Some days there was one request and some days there weren't any. But many days, there were three or four requests, especially if there was a renovation that was needed or a retrofitting or there was a new town somewhere or a new suburb, a new plot of land under development.

On one of these days, some days after the appearance of the Guard commander and the visit of the boss, the youngest brother found new requests in his inbox, requests for buildings that weren't strip malls.

"Firm's trying to expand the business," said one of the architects—one of the tall ones with glasses—while they stood together in the office kitchen waiting for coffee to brew. "The firm wants to reach into new territories."

To find new buildings unbuilt and to build them. It probably was, the youngest brother thought, that all of the strip malls that were ever needed would soon be built or were being built or had already been built, that if they continued, soon there would be no land outside the city that wasn't used for homes or roads or strip malls.

"We're remaking the city," the architect said. "Rebuilding it."

The youngest brother imagined a city that was all strip malls with strip malls for roads and strip malls for houses and parks and strip malls for stores. Strip malls at the horizon. Strip malls as far as anyone could see. No land not strip mall.

But it was in one of these new requests that the youngest brother saw the father's old factory. He saw the shape of it, recognized its fire-forged outline. There was something about this that felt warm to the youngest brother and he made a copy of the request and he kept the copy in the breast pocket of his white workshirt and it warmed him in the cold office.

Soon, there were other requests for the area around the father's factory, for the other factories and homes in the neighborhood that had long ago gone vacant but that still had some walls erect. He made copies of these too, not because of the father but because of curiosity. He decided there must be some development underway, and he looked again through his files for other requests to try to make sense of it. He made copies of every plan for the area and traced each building with his hands until his fingers smelled like toner and his nails dyed blue.

He asked the architects. He asked the receptionist. They knew nothing. He started drinking more coffee, spending more time in the office kitchen listening to the architects talk, filling his cup slower and slower, brewing new pots while the last was still half full, waiting. In the muddle of the earplugs he could hear only broad sketches. An adventure park for the area. Retrofitted structures and reclaimed forests and reenactment. Tourists. The war.

He went to the boss' office. The boss sat behind his desk framed in the ovoid gray of the clouded sun and the silent cranes and the unbuilt building in the window behind him. The youngest brother saw that on the upper floors they'd erected support beams and laid concrete, but the wind, which would soon drive snow, could still whip clear through each level. The boss looked up at the youngest brother, raised his eyes into the rounded rims of his glasses, the eyes of his glass lenses in the same shape as the eyes of the youngest brother's goggles.

The youngest brother asked about the project, about the park, and whether there might be a role he could play. He talked about the facility with which he handles blueprints and said, "In winter when it's windy, I could keep all the paperwork together. I could deliver important notes and keep the blueprints secured and the work orders and invoices pinned down."

"How exactly would you do that?"

"With rocks, probably," the youngest brother said. "Or with other things, depending on the vectors and strength of the wind and the weight of the paper to be held."

The boss smiled in a way that looked like he might laugh. He asked who would handle new requests in the office, and the youngest brother said he would do that too, promised to work overtime if necessary.

The boss thought for a moment and then said, "I guess there's some value in it." And the next day, the youngest brother was in the city again, working among the high-arcing weeds and trees and the crumbling falter of long factory land.

Their headquarters was a trailer with no windows and at the entrance there was a cinder block for a step and a door that would swing wildly with the wind. Before leaving the office for the last time, the youngest brother had made a file of all the blueprints they'd need and he rolled them into a tube and he set the tube inside the father's cracked leather gun case, zipped it closed, and slung the case over his shoulder. He carried the case with him around the worksite and, during breaks or when the blueprints weren't needed, left the case on a chair in the trailer.

At lunch, the architects would reserve tables at their favorite restaurants and they would leave the worksite in their cars, drive deeper into the downtown of the city or cross over into Canada or cross back out of the city to the suburbs. The contractors and the construction crew would upturn their helmets and eat out of pails. Some days there was beer. Most days there were thin sandwiches with no crusts.

When the worksite suddenly would go still and quiet like this, reminding the youngest brother of nights in their quiet house: this is when he started walking. At first he walked between bulldozers, from crane to crane, newly dug pit to newly dug pit. Then he found the long steel mesh and post border of the fenceline, the fence that enclosed the expanse of the park. And he walked along the insides of the fence, felt safe with the fence at his outside.

On one of his walks, he found a house in the same shape as his own house except this house had just three of four outside walls. This house opened at the front with only a skeleton frame, thin floating beams like a sketch where once there was a window and where still there was a front door off its hinges, ajar. All of its insides had been burned or scrapped. No roof, no glass, no copper piping, no interior walls to make rooms. There was a carpet of wild grass and fallen bricks and a board perfect for sitting.

The youngest brother in his earplugs and eye goggles entered through the door and sat on the board. As he ate, he looked up at the blue and gray of the sky. He heard the calls of his animals, the animals he'd named by letter, A through Z. And he imagined this city alive again, these city ruins and wild forest as tame again, and built. He remembered his transistor radio, the woman, the numbers.

The next day before walking the fence, he took with him the gun case of blueprints and a satchel filled with pens and wax pencils and chalk. And within the three walls and under the unroof of the abandoned house, he redrew the plans. He made space for the animals and the factories and he drew tall buildings next to thick forests, wind-bent reeds next to roads, smokestack plumes and salt mounds and wildflowers and graffiti like thick glass and steel. He drew a home for the father, a home for the oldest brother, homes for all three of their mothers, a whole neighborhood for each family. And when he looked down at the plans he saw he'd drawn an entire city, an entire world.

That afternoon at the worksite the architects called for the plans and the youngest brother went to them and unzipped the gun case. He pulled out the tube and unrolled the blueprints and laid them flat on a desk in the trailer, set smooth stones at each corner. The architects leaned over the plans, leaned close, adjusted their glasses. The blueprints were impossible to read, this half-finished park project now obscured by the youngest brother's marks, his lines and numbers, his factories, forests, and homes.

The next day was the youngest brother's last day as an assistant to architects, and for that day, in honor of the undead memories of the dead father and the dead mothers and the oldest brother, he wore his night black death suit and said goodbye.

## Part IV

Every night after the end of the war, the third wife would cook meals for four, set places for four. Four placemats and plates and napkins and forks, and she would sit at the table alone and wait for the youngest brother to come home. When he did, he would say hello. He would call her Evangeline instead of Mother, and he would ask, "What's for dinner?" as he'd stretch the tied strap of the goggles and scratch at his strap-matted hair.

The two of them would sit on either side of the table, the cut oak of it between them, and she would reach her hands low to her right and her left—toward the empty places—and she would bow her head and pray thanks for their bounty of food. As they ate, she would talk as she always talked, say the things she would say before these two men of hers died, before it was just her and the youngest brother. These dinners, the youngest brother was quiet, only occasionally looking up from his food and raising her into the roundness of his vision. Sometimes, if she went quiet, he'd forget she was there.

After eating, they would set off to their own parts of the house, she to the bedroom that was now only hers, he to the bedroom that was now only his, these bedrooms at opposite ends of a hallway in this, the only house left standing unburned unscrapped untagged on their block. There were parts of this house that were aging, near crumbling and that threatened to collapse on the youngest brother and the third wife. Roots from the tall maple had vined underground and had cracked the house's foundation. The maple's branches now touched the house such that it was no longer necessary to leap to the tree's trunk. If he wanted to leave in the night, the youngest brother merely needed to slide open the window and grab hold.

And when storms came, the rain and the wind would whipcrack the maple's wet branches against the soot-white siding, against the sill, and against the pane of the window in the youngest brother's bedroom. Some of these nights, rain would soak into the ground and ride roots into the basement. The rainwater swell would overwhelm the sump pump and the basement would flood. This flood was never more than an inch's covering of water, just enough to soak and rot anything left on the basement floor. In the mornings, Evangeline would mop the water into buckets she would carry upstairs and dump off the back patio.

Once, after a particularly bad storm, she mopped four buckets full, and rather than waste the rain,she took a shovel from the garage and, smiling and still in her night dress, dug a dirt shallow in the backyard. Bucket by bucket she filled her own backyard pond.

That afternoon, she put on a dress and her pearls and drove the family Plymouth to the pet store. "I'd like a dozen of your heartiest goldfish, please," she said to the sales clerk. "Package them carefully."

The sales clerk, a teen girl in a blue smock, said, "All the goldfish are pretty much the same."

"I doubt that," said Evangeline. "I'm sure there are little differences. Little differences are important."

The sales clerk scooped a long-handled net into the goldfish tank and swung it around until she'd caught what she could and she released the fish into a plastic bag. "They'll survive the ride home. I wouldn't expect much more."

"Thank you, regardless," said Evangeline. "I'll do my best to care for them."

Evangeline fed the fish every day, once in the morning after she woke and once at night before she slept. Sometimes she fed them fish food, sometimes leftover scraps. She added water to the pond, laced it with nutrients and botanicals. One morning two weeks later, though, she woke too late. The sun had beaten her to rise. Water soaked into the ground. Evangeline woke to find her fish laid out in a barren mud pit. All she could think then was that it had ended as she should have known it would. "It's all right," she said to the youngest brother at dinner that night. "It's all right. I expect good things. Sometimes bad things happen. Whatever. We shouldn't let them keep us from expecting good things."

In winter, snow would drift into mounds and weigh down the roof. Icicles would form, would cling to the rims of the gutters. Like always, there were early warm days, and on these days the snow would melt some and the icicles would dagger. Snowmelt would slick the sides of the house. And then the air would go cold again and the snowmelt would refreeze. The house would be coated with snow and ice and this freeze and unfreeze and refreeze would rust the siding where there was siding and splinter the paint where there was paint and warp the wood underneath it all.

In spring, runoff from the creek behind the house would run into snowmelt and together they would seep into the grass and the dirt and overcome the weary sump pump and leave the basement wet.

During dry days of summer, termites ate into the housewood and spiders built webs in the chimney, webs through the eaves, webs across windows and down dry rainspouts. When it was driest, when the sun was hottest and there was drought, the sun would glint off the spiders' silk threads and the house seemed wrapped in webs.

In this time, the neighborhood around the house began to disappear into the tear-downs and dust of the park project. The quiet of their city forest gave way to crashes of wrecking balls and jackhammers, to backup warnings and the swing of cranes. Traffic turned from dirt- and rust-colored family cars to bright yellow trucks. And the park's fenceline cinched closer, made their last block an island.

It was the fall after a dry summer when the youngest brother was fired and in the days after, rather than leaving the city for the suburbs or leaving their house for the park project, he stayed home with Evangeline. To him, she was the third wife, a mother-but-not-mother, his unmother. But to her, he was her last and longest alive son.

His first unemployed morning, he woke late and came downstairs to the kitchen, where she had prepared a plate of eggs and toast and a glass of tart cherry juice that, even behind the goggles, looked bright and red. The strip of photo booth pictures of the father was magneted to the refrigerator. Evangeline was at the kitchen table with a newspaper and a mug of coffee. Her eyes were warm, his were blank and tired.

Later, they sat at opposite ends of the couch and watched sitcoms and judge shows and old black and white zombie movies. Zombie movies used to be her favorite before the war. She and the father would watch them late nights after the oldest brother had left the house and the youngest brother had gone to sleep. Now they were bad memories and she sat through the movies quietly, as did the youngest brother, the both of them alone in the room together. The first night and the nights after it, they ate dinner together like usual, except these times the youngest brother tried harder to listen to Evangeline's stories.

She told one about when she was a girl and how she'd gotten in trouble for something she couldn't remember. "I didn't talk to my mother for days afterward," she said.

The youngest brother looked at her between bites. He tried to listen.

"Oh, I don't know." She laughed. "Looking at it now, now that she's gone. I guess I just regret it. I wish I hadn't wasted those hours. We could've done something together. Anything. It wouldn't have mattered."

The youngest brother only said, "I know what you mean."

Some evenings, they sat on the front porch watching the pyrotechnic exploding lights of the park nearby, these lights like fireflies: brilliant for an instant and then gone. Other evenings, the youngest brother took long walks with the sun setting, and he'd go to the boundary of the park, to the fence, and walk its edge until dark. She didn't like to leave the house and so she let him go. When he returned, he'd tell her everything he saw. On one walk, he said, he found a small opening in the fence probably made by vandals or scammers trying to sneak in for free. And he thought about getting low to the ground himself and pulling back the steel wire and crawling into the park, walking to the roofless house again and trying again to imagine the city he'd drawn. But it was dark already and he could hear animals in the city brush and explosions in the park and so he turned around toward home.

It was some time after this that the letters started. First there was one letter and then a week later there were two more. There was a fourth soon after, and it wasn't long before there was a letter every day. Each letter was on the same letterhead—heavy, crisp white paper with an address typed in small print along the bottom and a logo at the top, a black and white line drawing of a zombie. Each letter made the same offer: the developers were interested in purchasing the family's house and land. The owners of the other parcels on the block and in the neighborhood, they said, had already agreed to sell. But they, the developers, were saving their best price for Evangeline, if only she would accept their terms.

Evangeline wouldn't bring these letters into the house. "This is where my boys lived," she said. "Where my husband died." And so instead, she tore up the letters as they came, dropped the remains into a basket she'd set on the front porch for this purpose. Each time she would cry and each time she would say, "There is still life in this house." She would say, "There is life in these walls."

There was one morning in early winter when the developers came in person. They came before the youngest brother was awake. Evangeline saw them through the front window, and she went to the basement, to the top of the cabinet. Evangeline met them at the front door before they could even knock, they with their briefcases and file folders and checkbooks, she with her dead husband's shotgun.

///////////

They built it from ruins, this adventure park, from scattered foundry under forests of fallen trees and steel beams and sheet metal. It started quietly, with secret land deals that nobody noticed. First one empty factory was sold and then the factory across the street and then more factories and closed-up shops and bars and then houses. Tax liens and mortgages were paid off. Abandoned lots started selling in bulk. Lots with collapsed or collapsing structures were suddenly of interest. And those homeowners who remained got offers too substantial to refuse.

The park rose up from these city blocks. This land that once was populated and bustling, now valued for its regal barrenness, its exemplary resemblance to the end of times, a kingdom of the absence of everything. The absence of everything other than charred steel and broken glass, ash-blown weeds, and empty buildings.

Once the developers had purchased a big enough plot, they lifted the veil, brought in the architects and contractors and raised wrecking balls and cranes over the wild green of the low, empty city. They built a visitors' center and a hotel. A tramline. A gift shop. Old buildings were razed for parking and those left standing were reinforced, retrofitted to ensure none of the floors or ceilings or walls would collapse under, over, or in on the guests, these guests who would pay to fight zombies, to play apocalypse. All of this not in Muncie, where the real war began and ended. But in Detroit, which the developers found more suitable for the purpose.

Most of the zombies decomposed to the point they couldn't be identified and no one knew for sure whether they'd be dangerous and so the government had kept them secreted away in Death Valley. They offered the families of Muncie compensation and the opportunity to identify their loved ones and, if they could be identified, a choice as to how their loved one would go. Maybe out of shame or maybe out of some desire to keep whatever closure they'd achieved, most families declined even to try. After a while, the Fish & Wildlife Service decided to classify these orphan zombies as wild animals, wild game, and made them available for that purpose.

The park developers ordered a trainload of zombies from the facility in California and the train left Death Valley the same day. It arrived in Detroit one week later, the train slowing into the city's unused rail yard, past the abandoned trains—boxcars, mostly, made hollow by rust—into the central station. They herded the zombies through the station, through the lobby and its still stately pillars and columns of once-white marble, its high-hanging and empty settings for crystal chandeliers (the chandeliers, themselves, long since stolen), the wood-paneled ticket booth, the floorless levels and the glassless windows. This building through which hordes of travelers once had passed but which now was squalor.

They herded the zombies out into the city, into the park, guided them to the remains of a Masonic temple, to the temporary shelter they'd set up in the temple's auditorium. The stage, which had once hosted plays and concerts and commencements, was mostly intact, as was the auditorium's ceiling of filigreed tin tiles enclosing an intricate fresco of the solar system. But the developers had ripped out the seats, set up rows of army cots on the hall's long gray cement floor. The zombies marched unsteadily, filed into the auditorium and stood apart from each other next to their cots. And that first night, the zombies laid stiffly awake staring up at the ceiling, at the shimmer of the tile and at the deep black and distant gold of the universe.

They armed the first guests with nonlethal implements of destruction—water cannons and rubber-load shotguns and air rifles, nunchucks and aluminum baseball bats, mace. The idea was the zombies would attack and there'd be a fierce weeklong battle between the guests and the zombies. They staged a long pyrotechnic display at the gate entrance. Tall, booming explosions of free fire, all intended to be mortars of apocalypse. All to disorient the guests, to make them feel as though they'd been dropped into the middle of something real. Once all the guests were in, they closed the gate and let the zombies out of the temple, let them out to roam the park free. The zombies roamed free through the dark gray downbuild of the theme park ruins.

Except in that first week, there wasn't much of a battle. The guests were not well trained, many of them wealthy doctors and lawyers more used to working with their minds to heal or to resolve than to search out zombies to kill.

And the zombies were slow and seemed uninterested in conflict. Arms out, stiff-legged, roaming. Like they were searching, looking for something—whatever they could remember of their old lives, maybe. They shambled within the bounds of the park. Some found the fenceline and stayed near it, arms bent outward toward the river, the lake, the ocean beyond. Others seemed to nest. They moved toward walls and corners, anything enclosed. They gathered fallen branches and beams, huddled under torn roofs. There were zombies in the breakrooms of factories, in the backrooms of bars. There were zombies in the old state fairgrounds within the walls of midway stands or in gondolas of the ferris wheel. There were zombie families that formed.

The guests complained it wasn't real enough. That the park had promised a recreation of the war. That this was not the way outbreaks and wars were supposed to go. Park personnel pointed the zombies in the right direction and there'd be blood sometimes. But even after a well-placed thrust of the nunchucks, the zombies were still alive enough to move.

It wasn't long before the guests started sneaking in their own guns, shooting lethal ammunition at the roaming zombies. And it wasn't much longer until the developers started renting real guns at a premium. It wasn't long before zombies were shot dead for real, before they were forced over—before they were slipped over—into the land of the gone, before the undead started dying real deaths.

///////////////

Most nights the youngest brother lay awake and alone, the lit half of the moon inflected in the black crescent shadows of his eyes, shadows bounded by the plastic impression of the goggles. Most nights it was still, the only sounds the distant sounds of the park alive at night.

There was the night the sounds came closer. The youngest brother was in bed and he awoke to shouting. Mad words he couldn't discern. There were muted explosions, still distant and small and from the other side of the creek, but much less soft sounds the youngest brother could hear well, even through earplugs. The cracks of fire and flares.

And then there were sounds that seemed to come from near the house. He heard glass breaking. A hatchet's crack at wood. And then, a moment later, a blast that, in its quick, rattled for just a second the windowpane in its frame and the blown leaves of the maple. This sound, the youngest brother feared, had come from inside the house. He thought he could smell the powder. He felt the sound resonate. And the youngest brother recognized it immediately, this sound that so long ago he had named.

Still in his blue and yellow star-patterned pajamas and wearing the father's earplugs and eye goggles, the youngest brother stepped into a pair of slippers, reached for a flashlight, and went down the stairs to the first floor. He flashed his light through the living room and checked the back door, making sure it was secure. He searched through the kitchen. He opened cupboards and the doors to the pantry—for why, he didn't know. Out of instinct. To make sure nothing was amiss. He stepped into the laundry room and the garage, swung his light around the inside of the family garage. He looked under and inside the family Plymouth. He popped open the car's trunk and felt through the blankets Evangeline had stored there in case of emergency. He found nothing out of the ordinary.

Back inside, he heard movement from below, from the basement, and he paused for a moment at the door handle. There were emotions he couldn't quite fix. This basement was, to him, a place to go after things had gone, after events had happened. When they were kids, it was tornadoes—they'd go down there during tornado watches, take candles and radios and blankets, build forts to protect from the swirling wind outside.

Now he was afraid of the dank dark of it, the mysterious danger of it. What these sounds might betray. Maybe the oldest brother undead, brought back from war, back from death by whatever germ had started the war in the first place. Maybe the father. Maybe enough life had seeped into the soil to remake the father and maybe the father, undead, had dug himself out of the ground and returned here to this basement space. Maybe the youngest brother would have to see him dead again, find him shot open all over again. And he thought then: maybe it wasn't death at all that he feared, but this standing at the door, this in-between, this door open but unopened, this courage brave but not yet wielded.

He removed the earplugs and he pulled the goggles to the top of his head. And he looked down the short flight of stairs to the black gray of the basement, saw the cracked glass of the moonlight in a corner.

At the foot of the stairs, he surveyed the contents of the basement. He pointed the flashlight at the father's box of memories, which was intact. The father's workbench, hacksaw, toolbox, and vise were all in their right places. There was the unfolded card table onto which Evangeline had lifted boxes—Christmas decorations, toys, linens—above and away from the wet of the floodwaters.

Back past the father's cabinet, the youngest brother's flashlight beam snagged on something. Two short shadowed figures. At first, the youngest brother wanted to turn back toward the stairs, the door, to close it and call someone.

But instead, he forced himself forward toward the shadows, and there he saw two children shaking. As he saw them, the two boys stepped out toward the youngest brother, both with their arms out, one balancing the father's shotgun. It was laid loose on top of his arms near the boy's elbows that could no longer bend right.

The skin of their faces was peeled back and bloody and their teeth snarled. He could see skull. They looked scared and violent. They groaned a roar.

"Don't shoot," said the youngest brother.

The boys looked alike in more ways than the pale crisp of their skin and the uncolored glaze of their eyes. They both had black hair. Their hands were small and they stood the same shoulders-width and height. Their faces were similarly shaped. The youngest brother decided they were brothers and, even in the blank gray of their eyes, he could see they were not angry. That, probably, they were afraid. There was a sweetness to them. They must have, he thought, escaped, found the nearest warm house, broken in, and triggered the shotgun by accident.

The youngest brother relaxed his shoulders and spread out his arms, spread wide the fleece stars of his pajamas like he was the night sky. He said, "It's okay" and "I'm not going to hurt you." He held up his hands and their eyes, stiff and slow, followed the shine of his flashlight.

The youngest brother saw this and he shined the flashlight on his own face and then shined it toward the stairs and up toward the door to the rest of the house. He guided them with the flashlight slowly to the stairwell and then up the stairs and then into the muddy light of the kitchen.

Evangeline had heard the noise, had been woken by it, and she was in the kitchen when the three of them emerged.

"It's okay," the youngest brother said to Evangeline. His voice was a low soft he didn't know he could make. "Everything is okay. They're just kids."

They stood there, these four, for long stiff moments in the quiet flashlit dark with the moon light coloring yellow the white of the zombie boys.

At last Evangeline said, "I suppose we're all hungry or thirsty or something. I'm sorry I don't have what you'd like to eat. I hope toast will do." The zombie boys seemed to understand her and they both nodded.

The youngest brother guided the boys to the kitchen table. He pulled out their chairs and sat them stiff-hipped as best he could and slid the chairs close to the table. They rested their pale outstretched arms on the cut oak of it. The youngest brother sat too and Evangeline joined them with a plateful of toast and butter.

She and the youngest brother took turns buttering the toast and laying on jam and feeding the toast slowly to each zombie boy.

As they did this, as the sun rose and new sunlight filtered in through the curtains, Evangeline started talking, telling the boys her stories, and the youngest brother talked too, and together they told the zombie boys about their family, about the father and his wives, about the oldest brother, about the war and the memorial and the park, about their falling down house and what they might build in its place, about all that could happen now and that might happen now, now here in the last of the ever after.

ABOVE

# AIR RAID

We came back from my granddad's wake in a dust-smelling station wagon full of old things, his beat-up World War II trunk sticking out the open tailgate like a coffin. Mom and Dad had looped a pair of orange nylon straps around the sides of the car and through the back seat windows to keep it from sliding out. When we got home, Dad carried the trunk on his own to the basement and set it in a back corner next to the furnace.

I really wanted to open it just to see what was inside, but whenever I would even think of going down there, Dad somehow knew and did his whole "I forbid it" routine. It was a routine he did a lot. I was forbidden from going on dates even though all the other guys in my year had girlfriends. Just like I was forbidden from keeping the wagon out after dark when everybody else had cars of their own. Once, he caught me smoking in the backyard and smacked the cigarette out of my mouth. Nothing bled that time and the sting went away pretty quickly. There were plenty of other times when it hurt worse and I'd just try to shut it all out by imagining the ways other people have it bad too, try to make it seem like nothing.

But the trunk was this thing down there in the basement, this life force or whatever. It just kept beating at me, the strange coolness of it. Dad was always saying, "Some secrets need to stay secret." Except Granddad was dead and I couldn't see any reason not to check it out. I know he had a tough time in the war—sometimes he'd tell us stories about how he enlisted early on, how he saw all sorts of messed-up stuff in Japan—but it's not like he would've brought back anything too crazy, a skull or a live mine or something.

So one day, when Dad was at a conference, I went and jimmied the lock on it (same bad brand of lock Mom tried using on the liquor cabinet to keep Dad out). I don't know what I was expecting, but it was just old military uniforms at the top, which I suppose were kind of cool, and then further down there was a Colt pistol and a bayonet with spots of blood and rust. There was a canteen, too, a flag patch on some tan cloth, a helmet, and—this was the best—a hand-cranked air raid siren. It was green and the siren part was round. The legs of it folded over like a handle. I wanted to know if the siren still worked and for some reason I thought it'd be a prank to go out into the backyard and let it rip and see if I could get anybody to freak out. Sort of a *War of the Worlds* type of thing.

There wasn't much going on outside. The evil neighbor kids from across the way weren't out like they usually were after school and the sky was clear except for a couple of planes and the sun was hot because it was getting to be summer. I started it up, cranked it a few times, and the first note scared me a little. It was so loud and whiny, I was afraid it might distract the one plane flying low over the neighborhood, and I was worried it might be crashing or something.

I cranked anyway and the thing was screaming, echoing off all the houses. It had a music to it and the faster I cranked, the higher the pitch would go. I mixed it up with high and low and made a sort of song out of it. Three more planes came flying over. They were painted green and looked like old military jets, like maybe there was an airshow nearby, and I wondered if maybe they could hear it, or if maybe Dad could hear it, all the way downtown. Part of me hoped he could, that maybe he'd be annoyed by it, maybe it'd make his ears hurt. They did a circle and came back with a couple more planes and it was really happening now, this awesome siren I could make scream just by twisting a handle. Then another group of planes came in from some direction I couldn't see and they swooped down in a V formation, the siren still going.

That's when the bombing started, first on the other side of the neighborhood. The bombs whistled as they fell and the ground shook after they hit. I kept going with the siren, now more as a warning than anything, even though there probably wasn't anybody else who had any idea what it was supposed to mean. One of the planes flew right over our backyard and it was a second or two before our neighbor's house exploded into dirt and splinters and shrapnel. I remembered then that the evil neighbor kids were on vacation, so I didn't worry too much about it. I figured they'd just think a tornado came through or something while they were gone.

Still, I stopped the noise. It wound down into the low pitches like it was sad or dying. I figured Dad would say I'd done enough damage, so I put the siren back in the trunk where I found it and I never took it out again. I got one of the bad ones that night. He pinned me up against a wall so I couldn't move, couldn't do anything about it, really.

## AND I HAVEN'T DREAMED
## SINCE YOUR LETTER

That was the summer we got the idea to sleep with our heads touching in the hope we could dream the same dreams. Every afternoon you'd come over and we would lay beach towels on the lawn and set down on our backs, first looking up at the clouds and trying to call the same shapes. We would read two copies of the same book, same pages, same scenes. And then we would close our eyes at the same time, our hands across our chests and our heads pressed together like the two long legs of an A.

I could feel the grit of your hair and I guess you could feel the soft pulse of mine. On cooler days, there was the sound of wind through the leaves of our tall maple. And after a while we'd be asleep and in our dreams. Except no matter how hard we tried, no matter how many different ways we thought to do it, we always dreamed different things. I was at a meal in a city and you were lost in a forest. I was at a carnival and you were in a warehouse, an empty warehouse, dark, with slow-swinging light bulbs and faucets that dripped echoes. I was at a magic show and you were alone in blank nothing, floating in white like death.

I used to think we did all this because we thought it'd be cool, so we could tell all the other kids we'd found some secret escape into deep space, into the universe, to the stars, out to this other dimension of dreams that no one knew anything about. It wasn't until after you ran away that I heard the stories—first as rumors, and then I got your letter with no return address—about how there wasn't any right you could do at home, how spending days at our house was itself a way of dreaming.

I haven't dreamed since I started thinking that in those dreams we could've joined forces, could've dreamed an escape together—to a carnival, to a magic show, to a beach, to anywhere—could've dreamed an escape from the lawn, from the books, the clouds, from the wind through our tall maple, from the soft pulsing grit of our hair and our heads softly touching in sleep.

## OPEN MIC AND DRAFTS ON SPECIAL AND ALL THE PLAYERS ARE LOCAL AND BAD

Except a few weeks ago, guy walked into Ray's—shaved head, bucktooth smile, blue guitar—just stood there waiting 'til everyone else was done, then stepped up onto the plywood and started at it. Name wasn't on the list and didn't want an introduction, and I didn't get his name after, but he had to've come from out of town 'cause he didn't look like anyone and I never seen him since.

Can't forget that guitar, though: bright baby blue. Could say it was like the color the sky gets early April just after Easter before all the rain comes, that pure thin oxygen blue. My mom'd say it was the sky pretty-ing up for resurrected Christ and the late April rains were God mad at all us here on Earth for killing his baby son. Except at the time I wasn't thinking hocus pocus, just thought then it was the color of a workshirt I saw once at a Sears out by the highway.

I'm saying, this guitar was something different and this guy who I still never seen again, strapped it on, took out a pick, and just went to town on it. Banged out this savage tune to start that got everybody going. Amps at the sides of the stage weren't even turned on but the sound of that thing filled the room so full two of the sad-sack drunks down the end of the bar looked up from their drinks for the first time I ever seen. Started nodding and kicking their feet like this guy's busting out jolts of electricity straight into their toenails.

Then, for the second song, he got quiet, played off something soft and sweet, made me feel sick in the bottom part of my stomach. Made me remember that time in high school when I thought I'd found the one girl and I went to ask her out and she laughed right there in my face. While he was playing my face got warm, felt red, just like that day I'd tried to forget, that day all the love drained out of my chest. He was taking these loud breaths on the inhale, using them for rhythm in places you'd tap a snare or a foot. Couldn't help but breathe hard with him and before he was done my breath got long and cool and my head felt light and the bar felt new.

These local guys that think they're something, we usually cut them off after two songs. But wasn't anyone in that place that could move then, much less say something, and so he kept on for one more.

It was a miracle, I'd say, because that third song was the one. He stared off at the back wall like he didn't know we were there. But the hands knew and the guitar knew and his savage hands on that wild blue guitar tore right through us, drunks and all. I don't have a whole lot of words to describe it other than to say I've never been closer to thinking my mom was right—that right there on Ray's stage, in the sound of that Christ-blue guitar, there was some kind of rising, like the light shined down, man, and we all sang amen and all of us in that bar that night got our souls saved without even having to pay cover.

# HANGMAN

Kim was the one who found the guy hanging from an electrical wire and called the cops. She was walking to school but stopped when she saw him across the street. She said he looked like he'd been trying to steal copper, shears in his one hand, dangling from a low power line by the other. She said he didn't look homeless like you'd expect and that he was probably just a guy without much else going on and probably not a lot to lose.

It was almost the end of that semester and we all were looking for ways to get out of class or to make sitting through class less whatever. Kim and Zeke had figured out they could half-empty a juice bottle and fill it up with vodka without anyone really noticing and so that's what they did most days. At lunch we'd go out there to my old Lumina, just the three of us, and they'd drink and I'd smoke and we'd most days make it back into school for the last couple periods but some days not. I remember I'd been thinking at the time about all the different ways there are to die. The wire thing was a new one.

That morning Zeke and I were hanging out near the Pizza Hut on the white side of 8 Mile waiting for her—she didn't live too far over the line but 8 was as far as my dad would let me go—and Zeke was getting worried, I guess because he didn't want to miss class unless there was a good reason. Kim was pretty fucked up when she finally did get to us. Her eyes were all bulgy and her face was white. She kicked Zeke out of shotgun and said, "Drive," so I did.

I took us out toward the river first, where a couple of freighters were passing on the river and then back down through the Grosse Pointes by all the big houses and lawns. Kim wasn't saying anything and Zeke started getting bored and so I drove us back toward school when Kim started losing it and let out the whole story. She said she'd reached up and touched it—it was that close to the ground. Her dad was a cop in the city and had probably seen his share of bodies, but he'd always kept her away from all that, and this dead "it" was just right there in front of her and there was a part of her that wanted to see what it'd be like to kick it or stab it with a kitchen knife maybe, just to see how thick flesh feels. By that point she was really sobbing and taking long pulls from the bottle and she asked me to drive around some more, that she just wanted to erase the image of the guy's shoes at eye level. I knew it wasn't right that I kind of wanted to see it too.

Zeke said he didn't want to go to class and he suggested going down into the city instead, to an abandoned factory he knew, where we could all just do whatever. Kim said it sounded good and she reached across low and put her one hand on the inside of my leg where Zeke couldn't see and there wasn't anything I could do about it then.

The factory was on Grand near the highway and the overpass shadowed the entrance—a spot where the wall was crumbled a little lower than anywhere else—which made the whole place dark and wrong-feeling. There was barely a roof and most of the walls inside were only half-erect and tagged with graffiti.

They were taking turns with the vodka and I stopped to smoke and set my lighter down on a ledge. Where you could tell there'd been windows, now there were just empty rectangles. The city outside didn't look like much other than rubble, and I wondered how Kim managed to live in all this and still be shocked by seeing a dead man hanging from a line.

I turned back toward Zeke and Kim but they weren't there anymore. Kim was laughing far away, on the other sides of half-walls off in some other room. Zeke, I said loudly, but he didn't respond and I said, Zeke, again and then, Kim, and still nothing so I walked in and out of the sprays of light and the shadows with my Bic going. I said their names over and over and didn't hear anything except some lower pitched versions of their flat muffled voices and breath. I think the jagged stone walls must have warped in the echo whatever sounds were thrown at them.

I called Zeke's phone and, more than the dull distant buzz, saw the light of it raise up shadows of the two of them, their heads and bodies together, against a tall wall a couple rooms over. The bottle broke. And they were still on the wall, sometimes two shadows sometimes one.

Everything just fell then and fuck there was a big part of me that wanted to leave and drive back out of the city to where I was supposed to be. But I couldn't get my feet to move and I was really feeling the smoke, and so I stayed there and kept calling Zeke's phone and watching their wallshadows. After a time there were ragged gasps and a groan and the shadows stopped and I drove us all to school and that was all that happened that day. Though, I decided then that I hated Zeke and that I didn't like Kim nearly as much as I thought I did, and not just because she would do that with Zeke while I was right there, but also because in all she told us about what she kept calling an "it," a dead "it," she didn't once mention at all that he was once a real person who was probably trying to take care of his family and even though it was dangerous it was the only thing he could think of.

# IN THE SHAPE OF

That day it was cloudy and there was a grinding noise of gears coming off the clouds muscling into and out of each other, gears like on a car or a freight train but like they'd been winter-rusted. It'd been wet: cold and icy. And there'd been snow that fell for months and collected into white drifts made into mountains by the snowplows that rutted through our neighborhood. Just when it seemed the snow would reach to the clouds, scrape the bottoms of them, there was the big melt of spring, rivers of water rushing down snow mountains like villagers fleeing ash. Rain came, too. First we could see the clouds were heavy with it, holding it in by their grooves and swoops and swirls. But they couldn't hold it forever and eventually they gave way.

And I wonder if that's how it happened, those months of the mountains of snow, which to the clouds must have looked awful familiar. Like they held the snow once but never thought of it in that way and then looking down at the great piles of it, like looking into a mirror, like they'd let pieces of themselves fall without realizing. That the snow rose so high it almost came back: it must have been heartbreaking. The way sometimes you fill up with tears, but you dam them. And the new-formed lake of it all erodes your insides, corrodes, rusts, until you can't well it any longer. This must've been the clouds, all rusty and worn out and just trying to keep doing their job, trying to keep the sky working like nothing's wrong even though we all could hear different.

It was loud that day and most every day until summer came and then the clouds were gone and there was the sun and the road crews out fixing potholes with their orange barrels and their trucks of hot cement and tar, fixing up the streets while it was warm, before the next winter, before the clouds came back and it started snowing again.

# FINISHING MOVES
## [WHEN IT COMES CRASHING DOWN]

### Seated Senton

André the Giant in his car, a bubbletop CX Turbo made special by Citroen to fit the tall of him. He's got eight, one for each world wonder, and this one is stopped on the shoulder under a burned-out streetlamp, the cement body and billowing roof of the Silverdome a smokestack behind him, back past the circling blue and red. The match is over, all the fans are gone, the rush out of the lot done. His back aches and he can't feel his hands. His heart strains to pump blood to all the four corners of his body.

The cop is still in his car and has been for a few minutes. He said André was driving erratically, that that's why he pulled him over, and then he went back to his squad car with André's passport and registration. André thought about gunning it, screaming out of the shadow of the big place, straight through to the airport and back to Grenoble. No one would stop him. But he'd said yes to the kid, had him in the small of the back seat, asleep even after the cop lit him up with his flashlight, this too-tall kid that wanted to come with him, begged to come with him.

### Headbutt

When he was first starting out, he had the idea to fuck as many women as he could in the hope that they'd make giant André babies.

On the circuit in France as the Géant Ferré and later, in Japan, as Monster Roussimoff, and even for a few years after coming to America, in almost every town, there was at least one willing woman. He wanted to populate the world with Andrés. To raise up an army of Andrés. To conquer territories with Andrés. To rule an empire of Andrés where the small people were the ones everybody stares at. He gave it up after the diagnosis, after he was told his acromegaly wasn't likely to pass down.

After the show, André couldn't clean up fast enough. He didn't want to talk to any of the other wrestlers, didn't even care about driving out too early into the hundred thousand mass of people in cars. His suit still had that sweaty must to it, like champagne grapes would get back home if the vines were allowed to rot. The smell carried into the underground tunnel from the locker room—one end, the Silverdome floor; the other end, the exit, and he walked toward it as quickly as he could, which wasn't fast.

And then at the door and out to the ramp that led to the parking lot, where the kids were standing and waiting and waving, pressing into the metal barricade, a couple of security guys holding them back. The kids wanted autographs, the adults were shouting, throwing things, plastic cups and balled-up cards. André ignored them all except the one kid, taller than the others, thicker and rounder, with the same dark and oily hair. He had called out to André. His voice boomed at an octave André recognized. The kid called himself Andrew. He kept saying, "You're my father, André, you're my father." André had been to Detroit before, remembered sleeping with at least three women here, so he didn't immediately dismiss it.

He had security pull the kid from the crowd and together they walked up the ramp toward André's Citroen. The kid had a picture of his mother; André didn't recognize her. He finds them in every city, these big kids who claim to be his children, who want to run away with his circus. Most nights he dismisses them as frauds or as wanting things he can't give. But this night was different and this kid seemed nice and there was at least a little resemblance, at least a little chance.

"I feel so foreign sometimes," the kid said. "Not like the others." He grabbed André's hand and made him feel his neck, feel his stretching skin. André recognized the thinness of it, remembered how thin his skin would get, especially age twelve, the year he grew two feet. He looked down, saw the kid's giant shoes.

"It's not a happy life you're about to have," André said. "I can't help you."

The kid said he knew and that, still, he wanted to travel with André, to learn from him—not just about wrestling, but size too, how to walk through the world.

André smiled at this, the first time he'd smiled all night. Maybe it was the cold that made him invite the kid. Maybe it was the match, that look of pity Hogan gave him after it was all over. Maybe it was the sad thought of drinking alone in his hotel room, passing out on the too-short bed.

### Chokehold

That André could move well enough to unbuckle the seatbelt and stand was a small miracle. The cop said he smelled liquor on André's breath. In fact, André had been drinking: Crown Royal, two bottles before the match, two bottles after. It hadn't done anything. Made him nicer maybe, softened his heart a little. But Hogan's slam had hurt, rippled the brittle vertebrae of his spine. Now, outside on the shoulder of the road in the snowdark cold, all the cop can probably smell is the cologne André splashed on his chest, maybe the scent of soap from the post-match shower.

The cop asks why he wobbled on the straight line walk and André says, "My back," and, "It's cold." The cop doesn't get it. No one ever gets it.

"Where you headed?" the cop asks.

"The Westin," says André. His voice is low, rattles its own echo. "Downtown."

"This your kid?"

"Could be," he says. "I don't know."

The cop looks up at him with something like wonder. André sees this look a lot. The cop gives him the breathalyzer machine and it disappears into his hand like a short pencil. He wraps his lips around the tip of it. The cop tells him to take a deep breath and blow and he does, makes the machine whistle in the gust of wind, a gale it didn't expect. The Crown Royal doesn't register.

The cop says, "Wait here a minute," and walks to his car. When he comes back, he has a pen and a piece of paper and a camera and he asks for an autograph and a picture. "Guys at the station are not going to believe it," he says.

### Double Underhook Suplex

André the Giant on a bench in the locker room before the match, bottle of Crown Royal at his side. He liked to use the purple felt pouches to hold his valuables—passport, cash, rings the size of a man's hand, pills that don't work—while he's in the ring. It's a ritual: Remove the bottle. Empty his pockets into the bag. Pull the gold drawstrings. Set the pouch on the locker's top shelf above the gray suit he always wears before big shows. Sit on the bench and take the bottle in five sips. Always five. A good luck thing, as much luck as is involved in the outcome of a story already written.

Hogan came up behind him. Vince, the boss, too. They pointed him back toward a conference room. André knew what this was.

Vince was in a suit and he had a yellow legal pad that he set on the table between André and Hogan. Hogan already dressed in his rip-shirt and tights. André in his black unitard, a single strap over his left shoulder. He used to think it made him look like an ape but over time it had become more comfortable to him than street clothes, which never seem to fit right.

It was Vince who, just six months ago, came up with the idea for a "suspension," some time off the circuit for André to rest and heal. Of course he was the one also who, a month later, called André, pleaded with him to return, first as the mysterious masked Giant Machine and now, here, as himself again, as André the Giant.

He said, "Big Man, here's how we see this working out."

Vince and Hogan explained how the match would go. How Hogan would start with a failed slam, how his lower back would buckle under André's weight. He'd be hurt, play to the crowd, try to overcome the fake pain. Hogan and André would trade momentum, the advantage swinging back and forth until finally, around the fifteen minute mark, Hogan would go into his paroxysms. He'd Hulk Up. And in one last improbable and inspiring move, Hogan would—"Only if you say okay," said Hogan—lift André toward the Silverdome roof and slam him to the mat.

"It'll complete the narrative arc. A passing of the torch. A moment of pure beauty," said Vince in his sales voice. He knew André didn't like playing the villain and also didn't like to lose.

"You're André the Giant, man. I love you like a brother," Hogan said, "and I respect you like a father. The slam: It's your call."

André didn't say yes or no, didn't even say whether he'd take the loss, let Hogan pin him. He just said, "I'll think about it."

### Bearhug

In the light dark of the roadside with the snow reflecting the moon, André lays the sleeping kid in the backseat of the police cruiser, the last few steps pinching the buckling folds of his spine.

There's the match in Japan years ago. Before this Wrestlemania. Just André and Hogan and no security, nothing to separate them from the crowd, to keep the crowd back. There was provocation, of course, taunting. But something snapped that night. He's watched the video over and over: André the Monster stampeding into the crowd. The crowd terrified by the Monster, screaming, pushing through each other to escape toward the exits in frantic rolling waves. He's used to it now, the crowd's fear, but hasn't ever seen it caused in quite the same way by other wrestlers, the way water boils differently depending on the size and material of the pot.

Now, the cop hands André his coat to give to the kid and André holds it for a second and hands it back.

"Too small," he says. He pulls off his lucky suit jacket, bends slowly, and lays it over the kid. He wants to cry but knows he can't, that it'll ruin something. The story, maybe, so instead he watches the steam from his breath pass into the dark.

The cop and the kid drive off, disappear up the road, leave André and his car on the shoulder in the cold. It's one thing, he thinks, to be abandoned. Something worse to be unable to hide.

And so here he is, two months past his fortieth birthday, the birthday the doctors said he'd need a miracle to see. Here, this miraculous freak, this human Godzilla.

## Body Slam

Hogan rose from the mat.

All these moves André could have used, these flexes of muscle that lead only to ends of things, to a finish, to victory. André dropping a leg across Hogan's chest. André drilling Hogan in the forehead. André's hands, his elbows, his arms, the bigger-than-life of him overtaking Hogan and his smallness.

Instead: André yelling to Hogan under the force of the crowd: *Slam. Slam. Do the slam.*

He knew it would hurt his back, his heart. But he knew also it was time to do the only thing a giant can do: lose. It's been that way from the beginning, he thought. Since Goliath at least. Though this wasn't biblical. Rather, André thought of himself as a fairy tale. Like once upon a time, there was a giant who wanted nothing more than to love, but whose heart wasn't strong enough for anything other than a fight.

André widened his legs. Hogan lifted. André closer to God and then crashing down. Hogan on top of him.

One.

Two.

Three.

# WHITE SMOKE

None of us could figure out when exactly Annie's father emigrated from Poland, and the question came to be a joke he wasn't in on. We only knew it was sometime during the long bad time between the occupation and the roundtable. He carried messages for the Secret State during the war and, later, he changed his name and became a baker. Every time we'd drive down into the city, into Hamtramck, to his small house for dinner, it'd be warm and there'd be the smell of fresh bread or paczkis, and, at some point, he'd tell the story of where he was when Cardinal Wojtyla was elected Pope. Most times he'd call him "Cardinal" but other times it was "John Paul" or "John Paul II" or "His Holiness" or just "The Pope."

Once, after a few shots of his homemade quince nalewka, it was "Karol." I remember that night because I made the mistake of repeating the familiar, calling the pope by his given name, and my father-in-law smacked me so hard I thought a crown fell out. Annie was drunk too, and she sat in the corner and laughed.

But the story always started before dessert was served and it always started like this: "Every man and woman and child in Poland remembers where they were. You do this. You do this with your Kennedy, the day he was killed by that Soviet." Sometimes, especially nights when he skipped dessert and instead just propped back into his dull yellow-plaid La-Z-Boy, he'd digress into a full theory of the Kennedy assassination, about the Stalinists, about how the Kremlin could get to anyone anywhere. "I tell you I remember that summer. First it was Paul VI died. I think it was August. There was one John Paul they named and he died too.

This news was big. Big news in 1978." One time, I interrupted to tell him that was the year I turned thirteen, but he wouldn't hear me—once the story got going, he wouldn't ever stop. "I was here in Detroit, down the street from this very house. That year we opened the bakery. It was cold. All the people, they were saying the new pope would be an Italian or a German or some such. Some high family. We had a television in the back room. It was a big surprise. Little television, big surprise. This television, it never worked and I asked God for once to give us a pope we could talk to, one of us, and I swear I was saying Amen and it came on, the little television. Worked for once. Mother said the white smoke was just static. She was wrong.

"You know he went to the balcony. Popes don't go to the balcony, but Karol went to the balcony. Said these things about there's no such thing as a faraway land. All of us, all the people, one land in communion with faith.

"And then he was done and he went back in his castle and we went back to work. But I tell you, we all went to church that Sunday and every Sunday after, every Pole here, every Sunday." Except this last part about going to church only got told some nights and other nights he was already going to church all the time when the pope was elected, he was in a church when he heard, a church in Detroit. Or sometimes he was in a bakery in Krakow or a coffee shop in Krakow or at a card game or a bar, sometimes a bar in Krakow, sometimes a bar in downtown Detroit, one of those stone-walled bars that used to be a speakeasy during prohibition. The story changed depending on what we'd eaten and how much he'd had to drink.

Even Annie didn't know what was real; her mother, the only credible source in the family, died without passing it on. Though Annie said when it was just her and her father, he'd talk quietly about camping trips with Karol and the others, how they called him "Wujek," about their little family, how Wujek was more uncle than older brother. He told her he couldn't remember exactly when the Partisans had forced him out of his home and when he'd had to abandon the family name. He said he'd wrapped all those broken ends and pieces into the same memory and buried it deep inside, that John Paul's election, like a yeast, had made it all want to rise again and he drank every night to try to keep it down. I asked if her father really was related to the pope, and she said she didn't know, just that he and Karol must have known each other somehow and shared some bond, even if it was just coming from a place that didn't exist anymore and that they'd never go back to.

# KILL TV

They say the bunker is blastproof, that we're safe here under the desert floor, under six feet of reinforced concrete and steel. But every once in a while someone leaves the door open to the outside, and space in the bunker is so tight that it wouldn't take much to explode the whole place. It's just that it gets stale down here after so many days and there's this instinctual thing that happens in the body—the lungs, maybe—this automatic need for fresh air.

The operators don't ever actually go outside. Technically, they're not allowed to and for whatever reason it's one of the few protocols they always follow. Everything else is just a Middle East version of the Wild West to them. Like there's the operator we call Tex who yee-haws every time he pulls the trigger even though really it's just a button on a joystick. He's on Justine's team or, at least, the team Justine stands behind, and he always gives her this look before he does it like, *Hey Sweetheart, watch me waste this guy.* Like she'd be thrilled by that. Like it'd make her want to sleep with him.

Tex is flying on the big board now. Justine and Pete and I call it the Jumbotron, but all the operators call it Kill TV. It's early on a Tuesday and we can see the morning prayers and the throngs of people in the market halfway across the country. They don't know what happens on this screen.

Tex is a show-off, likes to fly in low, buzz the minarets, kick up some sand "to let 'em know we're watching." Justine has to remind him we're not policemen; we're supposed to be covert, stay off the radar. This time, though, he keeps it high to the outskirts of the city toward the coordinates they plotted in this morning's staff meeting. Once there, he flicks on the autopilot and sets it to hover on a two-mile-wide loop. The Con Man, the control room watch commander, flips to the video feed from the sentinel balloon we have floating up in the stratosphere watching an area the size of Alaska. He rewinds it, zooms in.

"Like I said. Right there," says Tex, pointing to a small dot moving into a house probably two stories tall. "He's there. Hasn't left. Miss Legal Sweetheart: Can I get a green light?"

"And we're all sure it's the guy on the list? That this is our target?" asks Justine. On her first day, she made the mistake of wearing a sleeveless blouse and we all saw the cluster of stars she has tattooed on her shoulder. I do some astronomy, and I think I was the only one who recognized it as the constellation Virgo. "We're sure it's him?"

"It's him," says Tex. "Been tracking him three days. We got facial from that ATM. House is empty. No collaterals. Green light?"

"Give me a second," she says. She's checking boxes on the matrix with her finger. This is Justine's third week and she's already said no six times. I've been with this group a year and said no twice.

"By all means, take your time," says Tex. "Maybe we ought to send you to work for the bad guys."

Pete tells Tex to fuck off, though Justine's getting better at handling herself, not looking rattled. She says, "Hey, I'm just trying to keep you out of jail. You'd be shocked how many creative uses they have for human heads in prison."

The Con Man, standing behind her at a control panel in the center of the room, gives Tex a look too, and the look is enough to back him down before he gets another shot in. Tex smiles with that long grin that reaches all the way across his face. He's the kind of guy you'd expect to have a bizarre, broom-shaped mustache, but his face is shaved clean and his red hair is buzzed and it makes him look unfinished.

Justine takes a deep breath, exhales, and says, "If we're certain it's him, I concur." She signs the kill sheet, pulls it off her clipboard, and passes it to the Con Man, who signs it and says, "Go."

Tex grabs hold of the joystick, maneuvers his Reaper back around toward the house, activates the laser-guidance system to "paint" the target, shoots that look at Justine, and does a loud yee-haw as he hits the trigger button twice and his chair vibrates, rattles the Coke can on the armrest. A cloud of dirt and shrapnel erupts on the Jumbotron and he shouts, "Score it!"

This is a new thing, the haptic vibrating chair. Defense Associates, our prime contractor, shipped them over last week, thinking they'd give the operators some tactile feedback during sorties, make it feel more like real war. The control room's relatively new, too; we were moved over here to AFCOM just a few months ago. Some guys had gotten too itchy and stopped waiting for go-aheads from Legal. Defense Associates thought being in-country would give the operators a better sense of the mission's gravity. Now instead of an air-conditioned conference room back home, we're all in a bunker in the middle of some desert—us and about three hundred computer screens.

"And that was a Kill TV shot," says Tex. "Two points, boys."

"Hold up," says Mighty Mouse, smiling and pointing up at the Jumbotron from the next station over. The dot is moving away from where Tex's missiles just struck and toward a cluster of buildings. "Look at that. Ha ha. Your guy's gone rabbit." One of the other operators yells, "Run, rabbit, run, ha ha!" and Mighty Mouse says, "Zero kill, zero points. Sorry, buddy."

"That's horseshit," says Tex. "I want another shot." He pulls his joystick back and then left, banks his Reaper around. Most of these operators aren't actually pilots but tech guys or policy guys or ex-military looking to cash in with the private sector. And there's so much demand now, HR had to cast a wider net to find some of the more recent hires—former hackers and gamers, laid-off auto guys, guys who've just been divorced or dumped and didn't have anything else, and even a performance artist. There's a written test they all have to pass to be considered for the job, and before they get a station and a Reaper, there's a whole course of instruction on flight training and etiquette. They let each guy pick his own fighter-pilot nickname. Tex, whose real name is Randy, owned a used-car dealership in Seattle before signing on.

The Con Man turns off the Jumbotron and immediately Tex turns to him and says, "Hey, put it back on. I'm taking another shot. Sweetheart slowed me down. No way he survives two Hellfires if she signs like she's supposed to. Put me back up. I'm dropping the five hundred."

"No way," says Justine. She looks back at the Con Man. "I'm not authorizing that."

"Like hell," Tex says. "I need these points. I can get this guy. I'm dropping a five hundred." He's flying a fifth-generation Reaper, thirty feet long and painted to blend in with the sky. In addition to the smaller Hellfire missiles, the Reaper carries a load of five-hundred-pound JDAMs that can each level a few city blocks. Except the big bombs almost never get used here. It's like throwing a hockey puck at a nickel slot.

The Con Man says, "It's over, Tex," in that quiet, low voice he gets when he's not sure about an order.

"Fucker is getting away," says Tex almost as a plea. The operators have a high-stakes game going. Each kill earns a point, and if the target is highly rated and the sortie's chosen for the Jumbotron, the operator gets two points. That is, as long as the mission is successful. When we first got here, the points were just for fun, but Defense Associates saw the value and started awarding bonuses based on point totals. It made the guys even more competitive. "You hear me, Sweetheart? Fucker is getting away."

"Fucker got away," she says. Two weeks ago, she wouldn't have cursed. She wouldn't have been so firm either. "He's in the city now. Too many collaterals, too many civilians. I'm your lawyer and your lawyer says no. It's done."

Tex looks to the Con Man and the Con Man nods and Tex says, "That's bullshit," and he turns back to his station and points his Reaper toward the next coordinates.

Once a month, Defense Associates flies in supplies and personnel on the corporate jet, new operators, sometimes to add to the crew they already have here and sometimes to replace operators who are burned out or seem unstable. We call it the monthly Reboot. With the hours and the stress, most of the operators are supposed to get sent home after two months in the bunker, but since they've had a hard time finding new operators, some of these guys have been here much longer. Tex is into his fourth month now.

The lawyers last longer. Maybe because technically we're not part of the mission; we're just here to make sure all the operators understand the law. Or maybe because we're not actually the ones pulling the trigger. Still, the lawyer who was here before Justine got a little too excited about the action and had to be sent home. He started to be an automatic yes on every target and he gave himself a pilot nickname, asked us to call him Wyatt Earp. In meetings, he'd get glassy-eyed and talk about the simplicity and beauty of the snaking vapors that trail from the missiles after they're fired. He wasn't wrong; there's a strange, intriguing power to what the operators do. Then one afternoon while everyone was in the mess for dinner, I found him in the empty control room swiveling in one of the chairs and pretending to pitch and roll and fire.

Any of that could've been forgiven. But he had his hands on the control panel and the joystick, and that's a clear violation of company rules. Crimes are one thing; even if a government somehow finds out, we have ways of persuading them not to prosecute. Violations of Defense Associates policy are serious. I felt bad turning him in for something we've all wanted to do at one point or another. But if I hadn't reported him, somebody else probably would have, and they'd have said I was just as guilty as him. The next day, Defense Associates fired Wyatt Earp and put Justine on the Reboot.


Justine's on the roof of the bunker when I climb the ladder. She's revealed to me in rungs: the high heels and the long flowy skirt and the official Defense Associates T-shirt the operators wear, a red bull's-eye with "Kill Shot" stamped across her chest, and the red sunglasses and long brown hair that strays and shifts in the moving desert wind. It's only 104 degrees, but it's early.

I usually only go outside at night, when it's dark, cooler, to track stars and planets and sky stuff with the telescope I brought. There's not much else to do here. But since she arrived, I've been up here more often during the day, started reshaping the landscape in my mind—still sand but with an ocean in the distance, the two of us alone on a private beach. Umbrella drinks.

"Saturday mornings were soccer practice," she says, picking up a conversation we started yesterday. I'd said something about the Jumbotron and how much more fun it would be to show classic movies or cartoons. "No time for Looney Tunes."

"Oh but there's so much more than Bugs Bunny and Hanna-Barbera," I say. "So much more. Serious dramas, 3-D, interactive cartoons, holograms. There're the sexy adult cartoons, cartoon porn." I mean this last one to be funny, but she doesn't laugh.

Something about being on the roof with Justine makes me want a cigarette, something to do with my hands. Inside the bunker, everyone smokes electronic cigarettes, whichever brand that pretends to burn blue at the tips and really just emits water vapor. The steam hangs in the air down there, makes everything feel hot and sticky-wet like Florida summers but without the Rollerblading and the tacos. Got so bad Defense Associates had to send over a couple of dehumidifiers to keep all the electronics from shorting.

"I don't know," she says after a minute. "It was just never my thing."

"Well, you missed out."

"I was more into video games." She sits down on the edge of the exhaust grate and air from the bunker blows up behind her in gusts, waving the back of her hair. She doesn't seem to mind.

"You know the machinery pretty well. Maybe in some alternate life you'd be an operator," I say.

"Maybe." She says this while looking down. At her feet there's a flower-patterned purse. She opens the clasp and pulls out knitting needles and a tangle of yarn.

"I'm kidding," I say. "You wouldn't operate. It's not you."

"Yeah?"

"They sent us your fancy résumé. Yale Law and straight to the bunker. Probably thought this was a fast track. Choice of firms when you're done. Six or seven figures for a while, pay off the loans. Then maybe something bigger. Something in government or politics."

"Sounds like you've seen more than just my résumé."

"No, I—I'm just saying, seems like you have ambition. Nothing wrong with that."

She's done a lot of work with the yarn, but it's collected in a weird shape I can't make out. Maybe a hat. She sees me looking.

"They're gloves," she says. "Will be. Knitting keeps me calm."

"Yeah. I'm sure I can see it. Nice."

Behind her, two camels crest the top of a dune and she turns to look too and accidentally stabs one of the needles into a palm and says, "Shit." There's no blood.

After a minute, she says, "You're mostly right, I guess. I mean, this mission; we're doing good things here. I just didn't think I'd end up in the desert."

I go to say something about believing in the mission too much, but Pete's black-gray hair and black sunglasses appear at the top of the ladder followed by the rest of him and I try to step him back down with my eyes.

He sees Justine, and then he sees me and smiles and looks back to Justine. "Just wanted to say: you did good in there. Didn't show any weakness. That's good." He's still married and sometimes when we talk about going on leave or about going into town or about what Justine looks like naked, I have to remind him what's waiting at home. He and his wife tried to have kids before he left, but they couldn't.

"Those guys don't respect what we do. They'll go for your jugular if you let them. But remember you have the power. Whatever they say, we have the power to shut them down."

"Don't think that I need you guys to back me up," she says. "I can handle it."

"We know," says Pete. "Of course." He lingers at the top of the ladder, one foot on the roof.

I want to be firm, tell him to go away, but instead I say, "We were—you know—kind of in the middle of talking."

"Oh sorry," he says. He smiles. He doesn't mean it. When we first got here, he and I hung a mini basketball hoop in one of the empty offices downstairs. Most times, I beat him. He's not a good loser. "Don't mean to interrupt."

Justine says, "No problem. We were just talking about stupid stuff."

"I'm sure," he says. Looks at me like he's won something. "Anyway, we all better get down there." Tries to herd us with his eyes. "Staff meeting in ten, right?"

Justine nods yeah and I say, "Yep. We'll see you down there." I look toward the ladder.

He takes a second. "Yep. See you down there," he says and then descends.

She's quiet now, her eyes on the needles. Her hands shake. We haven't talked as much since last week when I told her I love her. I knew as soon as I said it that I shouldn't have and I tried to backtrack and told her it wasn't a sexual thing, which was true. She still had some of that newness in her eyes and voice and she smiled and said I was nice and that was it. Pete and I have both wanted to tell her she should get out before she gets to be like us and now I'm thinking it may be too late.

"Why did your wife—"

"Leave? Because I was dumb," I say. "Still am. Just older and closer to retirement."

It's a thing we all have, the shaky hands. The operators run on thirty-six-hour megashifts fueled by coffee and amphetamines and the pure oxygen Defense Associates pumps into the bunker like a Vegas casino. We have to keep up or the guys might stray from the disposition matrix, the fourteen-by-seventeen sheet of paper laid out like a bingo card detailing all the circumstances in which a strike is authorized. It's our bible.

She looks up at me. She's annoyed or angry or sad or something—I can't figure out emotions anymore. "What?" she asks.

"Nothing," I say. "It's just—you're wearing the shirt."

She looks out toward the desert and then goes back to the knitting and I go back down into the bunker.


Defense Associates leases an airstrip half a kilometer from the entrance to the bunker. The airstrip isn't much of anything, barely long enough for the Gulfstream to do a tactical landing—a fast spiraling dive like a drill bit to make it harder to shoot at—and come to a stop under a sand-colored hangar that's almost invisible to satellites. From there, they airlift the supplies with small remote-controlled helicopters that drop everything into the bunker. And they tell everybody on the plane to keep their heads down and run for the bunker as fast as possible.

I was with some of the operators at the entrance to the bunker when the last Reboot landed so that we could help get the new people down the ladder quickly and that's when I first saw Justine. All the new guys were in military fatigues, but she was in a suit and a flak jacket and carrying a bag and she had a hard time running through the sand. But she smiled the whole time like it was fun, like it was a game to her, and it was the first genuine smile I'd seen (or at least noticed) since before I left home. Pete and I spent most of the next day showing her around the bunker, trying to make it look more luxurious than it is, and the rest of the day meeting with the Con Man and the operators explaining that though she was new, she had the same authority as Pete and me.

Even with our warning, the first few days were rough for her. Stick a bunch of guys in a desert bunker and they're bound to get lonely and competitive and hungry. For me, it was something else. That first week, all I could think was that she was exactly the woman I'd date if I could go back in time and do everything over again.

The afternoon mission is a scramble. All the operators team up with a spotter and each team gets GPS to a big target filled with people—shopping malls, grocery stores, factories. The aim is to rattle the building so that everybody inside flees. The operator flies in low and the spotters then, using Defense Associates' advanced imaging and identification software, scan the crowd as they're running. Once the spotter finds someone on the kill list, the operator paints the target, Legal checks the disposition matrix, and, if we sign off, he turns on the guns and fires. Plus one for confirmed bad guys; half a point for targets of opportunity, a.k.a. future bad guys; minus one for collaterals. At the end of the session, the team with the highest total wins a Defense Associates prize package. Usually just some gourmet food substitute they freeze-dry and ship over from home; sometimes a new pistol or a shotgun. The real prize is being king of the bunker for a few hours.

When we first joined Defense Associates, Pete and I tried to get them to stop doing scrambles altogether. This concept of targeted strikes against possible future enemies is an inexact science to begin with and the law's not exactly clear. There's always the chance that, even with sign-off from Legal, the operators could be charged in an international court. In scramble mode, it's tough for us to make snap judgments and sign kill sheets in time to attack. And there've been a few cases recently where the Defense Associates software malfunctioned and the algorithms gave false positives. Lots of negative scores those days. Even so, the Defense Associates higher-ups argued that scrambles are simply more efficient and effective than single-strike missions at neutralizing potential targets. Pete and I both worked at big firms before coming in-house and knew the politics involved, that we could only press so hard before it would bounce back on us, so we dropped it.

And I suppose there is something fun about a scramble. There's a buzz to it, an added electricity to the bunker. Like before a big ball game. The operators and spotters are all chattering and pumping each other's egos. The Con Man programs a scoreboard onto the Jumbotron. Some of the guys bring good-luck charms or take care of other superstitions, things that worked *that one time* and that they've been doing ever since *just in case*. Ghost Chili, a former high school teacher from San Diego, pulls out his too-big sombrero and everybody laughs. Tex, who says he's a Buddhist, meditates cross-legged on the floor near his station.

Eventually, the teams settle in and the lights dim and then there's just the hot glow of the monitors and the bright blue tips of cigarettes. The Con Man starts the countdown clock, someone does a fingertip drumroll, and at go time the operators all power up their Reapers and start them down the runway.

The first couple hours are anticlimactic nothing, just guys getting into position, piloting their crafts from Defense Associates' island air base six hundred kilometers out. There's the occasional "hoo-wah" or "yeah-boy." Once the operators reach the coast, the tension starts to build back up as the teams descend from cruising altitude, from above the clouds at twenty-five thousand feet, and maneuver to their designated coordinates.

There's an on-screen explosion and a "hell-yeah" from one side of the room, and just like that, the scramble starts going full steam. Screens show dust and dirt sprayed up and there are sounds of things breaking. The bombs, at least what we can hear from the onboard audio, don't sound like they do in cartoons with the whistle and the *kaboom*, though the result is essentially the same.

Somewhere on the country's other side in a city we've only ever seen on these screens, buildings rattle and bad guys run for safety. Here, there's a series of whoops and yee-haws and hoo-wahs. Guys in vibrating chairs swivel and twist, their bodies moving with their joysticks. Spotters spin remote video cameras to catch faces and scroll through computer screens to identify them.

Then there's Pete, Justine, and me. Every target requires a kill sheet. During our downtime, I went through a stack of them and prechecked all the boxes so that all I'll need to do is name the target and sign: yes, the target has been positively identified. Yes, the strike is consistent with the disposition matrix. No, the objective cannot be achieved by other means. Yes, the action is mission critical.

The requests start coming in and Pete's pen is furious and so is mine. Justine's trying to keep up. She flips through her book of executive orders, rereading the decision directives the rest of us have all memorized by now.

Tex is after her again. "That's a high-value target," he says loudly, trying to prod her to move faster. "That's a Kill TV target, Sweetheart. Two points, you hear?" She's underlining something in the book, working the check boxes on the kill sheet one at a time.

"Sweetheart, he's on the move. This is our chance. Let's go, let's go." I've been meaning for the last week to ask the Con Man to talk to Tex about his nickname for her, but the opportunity hasn't come up.

Justine's got a look on her face she's trying to hide behind her hair. Nervousness maybe, or something else. And I can see Tex's screen. The target's highlighted red, meaning it's a particularly cherry target, this red dot moving between buildings.

"Come on come on."

"I'm working on it," says Justine.

After a minute, the dot disappears into a minaret. "Shit," he says. "Shit shit shit he's gone. You fucking lost him."

"I didn't lose him," she says. She goes to take a sip of coffee, but her hand is too shaky to lift the cup. "He's not lost. He's in there."

"It is done, Sweetheart." It seems like all the action has stopped and everybody's watching her. Or maybe it's just Pete and Tex and me watching. The other guys are watching their scores, still working their targets. "Weak," says Tex. "You're fucking weak."

"Tex," I say and Pete says it too at almost the same time, just after I get the *t* out. "That's not—"

Tex keeps going. "Bad guy gets to go free and keep being bad, gonna get to kill some poor kid in Nebraska or Kansas or somewhere thanks to you," says Tex. Justine's head is down. "Little Bobby playing Cowboys and Indians with his buddies in the backyard. *Kablooey*—he's hopping on one leg and carrying a severed arm back into the house."

"Tex—" I say.

He goes back to his screen. "Might've been a football player or a president or a fighter pilot. Might've been your own kid. Sweetheart's little baby. Hope you can live with that."

The room is quieter now and when Justine finally looks up, her face is red and her eyes are red too, like there's something in her that's been bent close to breaking. She looks like she doesn't know what to say, her mouth half-open.

And then, from the back of her throat, she says, "Take the five."

Tex swivels in his chair. "The five. You mean the five hundred?"

"Yes. Authorized. Go."

Tex looks to the Con Man. He shakes his head no. Tex smiles. "I appreciate the new balls, Sweetheart. But that's a holy building. That's a no-go."

"Do it," she says. Tex doesn't move. Just stares at her. "Tex," she says, harder and louder than I think she intended. There's some shakiness underneath it. Maybe from the moment. Maybe from the amphetamines. "Take the shot."

"Belay that," says the Con Man from behind her.

Tex says, "I don't shoot houses of worship."

"Such morals," she says. One thing I love about Justine is how she gets tougher when she's challenged.

"I think you misunderstand, Sweetheart. I don't work for you. I work for the Con Man. I fire on his orders. You can stop me, but you can't start me."

Her eyes are fierce now and she's more of an angry red. She goes to his station. Pete follows. "Fine," she says. "Then I'll do it." She grabs for the joystick.

"Justine!" I shout from across the room and Pete puts his hands on her arm and her shoulder, stops her hand just short.

Her lips are shaking. Mine are too.

"Then it's on you," she says to Tex. "Your fault. You're weak."

Pete tells her to go back to the barracks and then it's done and he and I finish the scramble for her. Mighty Mouse wins with fifteen points. "You got lucky," Tex tells him. "You got a fucking bad-guy convention there."

Mighty Mouse says, "It was all skill." And then things quiet down and the guys land their Reapers and retreat into the mess for beer.

The air outside the bunker is black and yellow with a quarter moon and as many stars as maybe there've ever been in the sky, like lights left on, like they're saying, *Someone's home* and *Come on in; you'll be safe here.* Justine's sitting on the exhaust, yarn spread out at her feet. I don't know how she can sit out here and not look up.

There's a quiet that's not really quiet.

"The thing about Bugs Bunny," I say, because it's all I can think of that might help, "is that he's kind of an asshole and he gets away with all kinds of shady stuff just because he's got this reputation as a nice guy."

She laughs without smiling. "Give me an example."

I take a minute. "Yeah, I got nothing. It's been too long since I watched."

"You have kids, right?"

"Two girls. Nine and eleven."

"Girls are the worst," she says. "I couldn't do it. I'd be horrified they'd be captive to false gods—Disney and boy bands and Facebook."

"Luckily they're over that stuff. Now it's more graphic novels and robot pets and 3-D printing."

"They don't know you do this."

I tell her no. There's no point explaining.

"You know they'll still love you either way, right?"

It never feels that easy, I think. Never.

"Law is all I ever wanted to do," she says after a minute. "Never fireman or astronaut or anything else. Just this."

"Seriously?" Few of the lawyers I know want to be lawyers, much less corporate lawyers.

"Not this exactly. But, you know, real law. Something where I'm helping people. Not marking them for death."

"No." I want to say, *There's a big difference between us and them.* "We do good here. Make sure the process works. They're the ones who do the shooting."

She says, "Yeah," and then again there's the quiet that's not really quiet. Far away there are explosions and sirens going. And the sound of the night dervishes whipping through the sand and the sky so fast only a miracle keeps the stars from moving the way everything else seems to. Still, she's there with the shaking hands and the knitting needles. "Maybe now they'll listen to me."

I want so badly for her to smile my teeth hurt. I want to say something, to tell her something original and important. Except I don't think there's anything I know anymore that she doesn't and so instead I go back to the telescope and move it a few clicks over to a different spot. There's a moment, maybe from the heat, when the stars seem to fire light through the lens, make us glow red. And I pull away from the telescope and turn back toward her. "We should get back down there," I say. "Staff meeting for tomorrow, right?"

She looks up at me and says, "Yeah, I guess so," and does a last loop with the yarn and then pushes the yarn and the gloves and the needles into the purse and closes the clasp, and I let her go down first before I go too, before we both disappear back down the ladder into the bunker.

# THE PILOT

*(after Russell Edson)*

There's the old man alone in his room and up in the dark of the dirty window there's the light of a star. He stands at the back of a chair, the chair a captain's wheel, he thinks, the star repeating cycles of nuclear fusion exploding light and dust, the room stardust. He steers the room by this star, steers through the night, steers until the starlight fades and falls behind the black of a cloud. First there're the advancing drips against the roof and then the long drops that draw tears on the pane and then the rhythmic flood. The rain a waterfall now, and he says, "I am afraid." The hazard of this night waterfall, that there's no seeing the width or depth of it, the height.

He says, "Be brave, my Captain."

Like the first explorers, who sailed to the edges of the world and who, from fear of falling, tied long lines to stay moored to the shore and who, when the lines ran taut and snapped, continued regardless.

Like the first fliers, who chased groundshadows after gliders and who laid down pillows to avert disaster.

Like the young boy, who dreamed of stampeding through the atmosphere on a bed, reaching his star, catching it in a lasso, bringing it home, keeping it as his own.

From this memory, the old man thinks he can steer through the dark of the clouded star and into the hard mist of rain to the base of this waterfall, throw ropes around rocks at the head of it, form pulleys, lift and steer the room into the sky, up and over the rain.

"Be brave," he says again.

And with all his strength he pulls his room into the wet dark of the night air, into the clouds and beyond.

# AWAY

# FIREWORKS

### Fourth.

We were on the granite coast with the sun going down and the fireworks starting. There was the park with the army-green grass faded in the dusk and you and I were on the swings watching new stars shoot out over the ocean and you said you'd never seen those colors before. I didn't believe you at first. I said every kid's seen sparklers against the red sun, even kids from the desert. Though as soon as I said it I realized you weren't watching the sky. You were looking at my cheek, which was bruising blue into purple and black.

### Third.

They left me at the edge of the cliff above the beach while, below, they lit dazzlers and fountains and roman candles, shot yellow globes up into the gray. It was beautiful but seemed like a waste, all that money and whatever just for a few seconds of skyglow. Then you were back with light in your hand, like you'd caught one and saved it. You had a towel and dabbed at my forehead, kept saying you'd never seen anything like it. That's when I thought this might be something.

### Second.

I thought I had it wrong when you went back inside without saying anything. You had that look, both at his vincible wreck and my bleeding lips, one of those last looks like you were storing the image of it—our sweaty hair and the bruised ground—to remind yourself never to go through this park again. The others thought it was all so funny, the way he and I went at each other, our lousy ocean legs and arms swimming slow. But my chest felt like you'd gotten a shot in before you left, knocked the wind out of my lungs.

### First.

There was the guy who thought you were his, grabbed at you with words and hands that'd worked with other women. I stepped between and he got mad and there we were in the park near the swing set and the sandlot with thick red gloves swinging drunken punches. They circled us; you sat on the low end of the teeter-totter. I clipped the side of his head and he followed hard with a right. I fell backward, recovered, came running at him, and didn't stop when his hair hit dirt.

### Zeroth.

We were the only ones awake in the early morning house. I made coffee, asked which of our common friends you were with. You said no one. There was that smile. We ate eggs on the porch as the fog burned off and we wondered if you could see the fireworks from space, whether the moon would feel lonely in its orbit, would strain to reflect their firelight the way it reflects the sun. Or whether the stars could be jealous we replace them so easily—just gunpowder and flames.

# EXTINCTION EVENT

## I

They had to have seen it coming, there in the humidity of the primordial swamp. Science hasn't pegged an IQ on the average dinosaur, but triceratops had smarts and at some point one of them must have looked up and thought, *Hey there's a giant round something headed our way; that's not good.* They at least had instincts and what instinct is there in that situation—the situation of watching a city-sized ball of rock deathangeling through the heavens—other than to gather a few friends, like stegosaurus and pterodactyl, maybe, and T-Rex with his slim but lithe baby-arms, and to build a generation starship?

## II

There would've been a plan of some sort, a team of dinosaurs wearing lab coats and safety goggles and gathered in a circle around an arrangement of rocks in the shape of a space vehicle. There'd be a construction phase and training in which the chosen few heroes of dinosaurdom simulate flight conditions while the prehistoric rocket is assembled. And then those last few moments before liftoff: the sun blacking in the sky, the dino-astronauts waving goodbye in their last earthbound moments, their tail-shadows subsumed by the shadow of the hurtling rock. There's a point, there in the ship as they rise up through the atmosphere, when triceratops looks back at the Earth. His ceratopsian hoof waves, touches the window, lingers.

III

The impact shuddered the world, dented a crater ten times the rock's size, triggered a skyscraping tsunami that wiped out most everything in its reach. Earth fell into darkness from dust kicked up into the stratosphere and kept floating there in gravitational limbo. There were fires and acid rain.

They didn't all die at once. Death came in waves. The flora were killed first, starting the vegetarians on a death spiral. Then the carnivores turned teeth on each other. Eventually, even the scavenging carrion-eaters went hungry and passed.

IV

The surviving dinosaurs wouldn't have known any of this from space. They could only imagine. And if dinosaurs had any capacity for guilt, it would have been tremendous. *Why us?* T-Rex might've asked himself, alone outside the ship repairing a solar panel and looking back toward Earth, his flat-jointed neck strained against the insides of his dino-shaped spacesuit. It's only when we're most lonely that we think so deeply about others. *Why do we get to live while everyone and everything we love dies?* Their ship would've zoomed on regardless.

V

Somewhere now there's a ship full of dinosaurs cruising through space, all gap-toothed and rickety genius thanks to a couple hundred million years of inbreeding and evolution. Or maybe they found a hospitable planet, set up a civilization, built a small world of their own. Maybe they gather on the anniversary of their launch in the first light of some new star, circled around the morning shadow of earthly monuments made to remember the dinosaurs they lost and the extinction they were fortunate to survive.

## ROLLO IS ROLLO

My brother Rollo shows up the day after Christmas with an unwrapped box of Legos and a Meijer bag carrying underwear and a dirty flannel. Still on the porch, he hands me the box and says, "It's for the kid." Neighbor up the street in her bathrobe out picking up the newspaper and salting last night's ice, watching. Rollo says he found it in a store and that it "just reminded me of her." This, after Jenny, our two-year-old, hasn't ever seen him in her life and I haven't seen him in I don't know how many years more. She doesn't play with Legos, she eats them. I guess there's no reason for him to have known that. Just can't picture him doing anything other than taking whatever he could grab from the Toys for Tots box before peeling out of some grocery parking lot in that rust-red Ford Fiesta he's been driving since Mom died.

I never know what to say to my brother.

I tell him, "Everyone's asleep." Jenny's upstairs in her crib and Emily's napping, too, if the dogs didn't wake her up. They heard a car door slam and started barking, maybe out of fear, maybe out of intuition. I was asleep, too, spread the length of the couch, until the doorbell and the dogs. It took a second ring for me to trust I wasn't dreaming and another couple minutes to get up and pull on pants with my one leg feeling crooked.

He says, "I get you're not excited. But at least invite me in?"

"I'm happy to see you," I say. I lean in the width of the doorwall. "Just didn't expect to."

"Do you ever expect to?"

"No," I say. I resolved to stop expecting things a long time ago. During one of our worst fights, Emily said it's why I'll never be satisfied. "Not really."

Rollo says, "Fine. Buy me breakfast, then."

And, if only because it's the quietest way to get him off the front steps, I say, "Okay," and tell him to wait while I grab my cane and leave a note.

Two other cars and a homeless guy in the parking lot of the Big Boy, and, inside, the waitress looks like she hasn't slept in a week. She glances up from her cell phone and points us to a booth in the corner past the salad bar that's all brown lettuce and empty metal trays. I let Rollo sit with his back to the wall. He likes to be able to watch the door.

He's got this smile, all angled teeth, fewer missing than I remember, and his usual red eyes. There's a bruise on his neck and he's been cutting his own hair. It's blonde and looks chopped up. It's a bad sign. He waits for the server before he'll start in, I'm sure, on whatever his new thing is going to be. She asks how he wants his eggs.

"Three of them," he says. "Over medium. And an order of bacon. Pretty please." He shows her the smile, introduces himself, calls her by her nametag, and she buys it. I want to tell her Rollo isn't even his real name. That his real name is Mark. That he lies when he tells people why he changes it. He has this line about it being a Malcolm X thing, some brand of self-expression, choosing his own identity instead of the one he was born with. Really, it's that he's been kicked out of everywhere he's ever sat down—schools, bars, our house—and he started doing it out of some combination of anger at our parents and fear about having to pay for the things he steals. He picks a new name every few years, every time he needs an alibi or an escape. Like a new name changes him somehow. Rollo's lasted the longest. But whatever his name, Rollo is Rollo and that's not someone anyone wants to be.

The waitress doesn't know Rollo and didn't know him last time he showed up looking for something, much less when we were kids, and so instead I just tell her, "I'll have coffee and toast."

He sits back, arms out across the back of the booth. "I was thinking the other day about you and me," he says. "That time I took you for your first drink. You were fourteen. Remember it?"

"Hell of an older brother," I say.

"I got you that fake ID."

"I remember it."

"The name on it—it was something foreign. Francois or something. You thought the guy in the picture looked fancy so you put on this whole character. Like they'd think it was a fake if you weren't foreign." He laughs and his chest slips into a cough. "'Yessir, I would be well pleased if you'd make me a gin and tonic.' Beefeater. Because you thought that's what the guy would've wanted. Remember?"

I say, "I remember" again. It stops him for a minute. He leans back as far as the booth'll let him, looks around the place, settles on a brown spot in the ceiling tile. Still with the smile and the eyes. Like a deer or a dog.

"Rollo—"

The waitress comes up behind me, interrupts, drops two plates between us. Rollo bends over his plate, gets his nose over it. His hands shake and he has a hard time cutting eggs with the edge of his fork. The homeless guy in the window across the way trying to light a cigarette with a Bic in the wind.

"Rollo," I say again, and I ask what's up, why he shows up the day after Christmas with unwrapped Legos and a Meijer bag full of dirty clothes.

He tries to steady his hand through the handle of the coffee cup but it just ripples the coffee. Like sonar. "It's been a couple of months now. I didn't want to see you—to see anybody, really—until I had time to, you know, time to process it."

I say, "Okay."

"From what I know, it wasn't more than a night I was up there. Could've been more. It seemed like a lot longer, like a year maybe."

"Up there—"

"Yeah. But, so, I'm driving out in the country. Outside of Grand Rapids or one of those. In the Fiesta. It's late. And I'll be honest, I'd been in a fix. This road going through fields. I was staying with this girl for a while, some old abandoned house she'd squatted. Well I'd scored us some stuff in town and I was headed back to her except I didn't know the way. And I can't see real well at night anyway. It's just this pure black out." All slower than his usual patter. Takes a sip of coffee like he's trying to speed himself back up. "And right there in front of me, blocking the road, there's this big blue light that just comes on all of a sudden. Out of nothing. And it's the only thing I can see, this bright blue light.

"So I stop and I get out of the car to see what it is. And then that's it."

"That's it?"

"Yeah. That's it. Next thing I remember, it's morning. I'm on the side of the road. No shirt. My pants are ripped. Fiesta's still got its lights on. Like I blacked out, except not like that. Like there are things I remember that happened, but it was someone else that went through it. Except I know it was me. It had to have been.

"It's these flashes of things—like there's a zapping sound and there's a big steel door that opens up like on a DeLorean, down and up, like *Back to the Future*, but different. And then a waiting room with chairs and beds and everything's white like snow and really bright. Then I'm on some kind of metal table that seems like it should be cold but I can't feel it. I can't feel anything. And all around there're these alive things like nothing you've ever seen, maybe five or six of them, all green and glowing from their insides—"

"Rollo," I say. Every Rollo story ends with a punchline. He needs something or he wants something. It's just a matter of how quickly he gets to it.

"I know it's crazy. But just listen: They wouldn't do anything. They wouldn't touch me. They said I was 'unclean.'" He stops here, laughs, looks around the restaurant. I try to signal the waitress for more coffee but she's not looking. "Next thing I know I'm in the ditch at the side of the road all covered in piss and blood and just messed up. And here"—he sits up in the booth, pulls up one side of his shirt—"when I woke up I had this scar," he says, pointing to the underside of his ribcage. Below the thin outline of his ribs, there's a patch of skin, maybe two inches long, darker than the pale rest of him.

"Wait," I say. "Isn't that from the fight that got you kicked out of high school?"

"No," he says, "you don't understand. It was them. I got this from them. I had it when I woke up."

"I don't—"

"But how shitty is that?" he asks. "Get abducted by aliens and they wouldn't do anything. Wouldn't touch me." Except to give him a scar he already had, I think. "Like they're too good for me. I mean, I know I'm not the best specimen of humanity, but shit. There's nothing they can learn?"

I keep my eyebrows low in case he thinks I'm actually believing him. I ask, "So you're upset because you weren't probed?"

"I guess—I know when you put it like that, when you say it like that," he says, "it sounds strange."

"Yeah."

"It's just, there's this thing I hear when it's quiet now—you know, like some people hear ringing in their ears—it's: 'Be clean.' And that's it, over and over. I don't know if it's something they implanted in me or if the scar means something or if it's something I just suddenly started saying to myself or what. Whatever. It's just caused this revolution in how I think about things and about people."

"Good," I say, probably more dismissively than I should. "I'm glad." He's had these "revolutions" before. He changes his name and makes a list of new ideas and they stick for a month or two until his pathological whatever kicks back in and retakes control.

"No, you don't get it," he says. "I tried to kill myself after this. I went on this epic, epic bender. Tried every kind of shit I could find. More than before. And I couldn't do it. I couldn't die." Still not sure I'm believing the story, but it's something we talked about a lot as kids, suicide. What gets someone to the place where they'd rather be dead than alive. I've thought of Rollo as doing it slowly, wasting himself away until he's all gone, until the night I get a call to come identify his body out of some backroads ditch. Sometimes I wonder what it means that we came from the same parents and, because we did, if there's a ditch somewhere for me too. And I look down at my coffee and my hand is shaking now too, and I think maybe it's not me, that maybe instead it's the world that's shaking, the whole world in tremors, like that theory of the universe that we're all just piles of vibrating string.

"I need your help," he says now. "I've been working at it. Trying to get myself better. Checked into a facility for a couple weeks." He waits. "I want to be a firefighter."

"A firefighter?" Like he's five years old.

"Just listen." He leans over the table. His breath is stale coffee. "I need you to tell me something. Tell me I still have time to be a good person. That I can still make everything up to everybody. Everything I've fucked up."

"Rollo—"

"I know. I know there's a lot. Just—"

My hand is still going and my neck is warm and I can't think of anything less honest, so I say, "Rollo, I haven't seen you. I don't know what you can and can't do anymore."

It stops him. "No," he says. "I know." His lips close and his eyes get small like they used to when he was little, when Mom was still alive and she'd yell at him for what he'd done and he'd run off to our bedroom. Back before he gave up on guilt. "But it's never too late, right?"

There's something in me that doesn't want to say "yes" even though I know I should. All I can think of is the day Dad kicked him out, the day he crashed into the living room—the sound of it—and I'm there in front of the TV with the Fiesta coming through the wall, pinning my leg.

And so I say something short about having to work at it and having to earn things. I say, "It's not just money you owe."

And the waitress comes back with the bill and my credit card and I sign the slip. Rollo looks up at her, puts the smile back on, and says, "Thank you very much, beautiful. It was great."

Then we're outside in the parking lot. It's warmed only a little. The sun is bright off the ice-crusted mounds of plowed snow in the corner of the lot. Past the Fiesta there's the homeless guy—beard, sunken eyes, thin—walking along the road toward the crosswalk. It's one of those big intersections of main roads and he looks unsteady as he presses the button to call for the walk signal. And he looks over at us and up at the giant plastic red-and-white statue of Big Boy holding a hamburger. He starts to shake and his eyes come back down to ours for a second before he goes to one knee and down onto his back, half in the snow-covered grass, half in the sidewalk.

Rollo says, "Shit. Looks like a seizure. Call someone," and he takes off toward the guy. The waitress sees it through the window and comes outside with her phone and I can hear her talking to 911.

Rollo moves the guy onto his side. Pulls off his own jacket and puts it under the guy's head, cradles the guy, tries to keep him calm. Like a pro. Me, I just stand there. Never had any training. Nothing I know to do. Main thing I notice is Rollo's coat soaking up the foaming drool coming out of the guy's mouth and I feel faint because of it, sick, and I hate myself for thinking it's gross and for not knowing how to help. Can't remember ever seeing Rollo move so quickly before, at least not since we used to race each other as kids. I guess it's only recently I started thinking of him as gaunt and brittle. Somehow, in my mind, his body is easily cracked.

The guy starts to flatten out and the seizure stops and Rollo tells him to take deep breaths and he keeps his arms around him, keeps the guy's hair back and strokes his forehead. There's something about it that's beautiful and it's a beauty that's almost religious: a man on his knees, sweating, face lit up by the reflection of the sun in the melting snow. That it could be anybody.

Rollo keeps the guy on the ground until we hear the sirens coming and the ambulance pulls up and the EMTs take over.

He walks back to me and the Fiesta. I don't know why I expect him to just put the spit-soaked coat back on, but he holds it out away from himself and tosses it in the backseat next to the Meijer bag.

Rollo turns over the engine and puts the heat on full and I look at him. I can't think of the right words—like all at once there are a million things I could say and none. What comes out is: "Get all that from the little green guys?" And immediately I feel stupid.

"Seriously?" he asks. He lowers his window a crack and lips a cigarette into the red coil of the car's lighter. "I've seen a lot of overdoses, man. Some of these facilities too: everybody's coming down, bodies are fighting it. You learn all kinds of stuff. They have classes."

We drive back to the house and get halfway up the walk and I can see Emily in the front window. She's crossing through the kitchen and she looks out and sees me and sees Rollo and she gives me a look—we know each other so well—like we've talked about this before, that he's not allowed around our daughter. We've argued about him a lot. It was me who convinced her he was dangerous. Now I don't know. I look back at Rollo. In the cold, in just a shirt with his shoulders hunched and his arms tight at his sides. Even here he looks bigger somehow.

He looks in through the window, pulls his arm up and does a half-wave before she disappears into the living room. "You married a beautiful woman," he says.

"Yeah."

"How's she doing?"

"She's good," I say.

"Good. You two are good?"

"Most of the time. Yeah."

"The leg?"

"Yeah."

And then it's quiet. Just Rollo and me. There's a moment where he feels like a big brother again, like I could invite him in and it'd be different now. But all that escapes is breath and steam in the chill.

He does the smile and the sharp angles of his teeth snap me out of it.

"Rollo—" I say.

"No," he says. He looks back at the Fiesta. "No, I get it. It's okay. I told them I'd check back in before dinner."

"Told who?"

"The facility."

"You're still—"

"For now."

"Good for you," I say.

"Yeah," he says. "Take care, brother." He holds out his hand and we shake and he turns back to the Fiesta.

After a few steps, I start after him.

I say, "Rollo," and before he can turn, I put my arms around his shoulders. I cross my hands at his chest and he leans back into me and I put my head against his. He presses back into me and I drive my chin into his shoulder and I hold him there, both of us still for once. He smells like soap and for some reason it makes me smile.

I let go and he gets in the car and then there's just the sound of the tires of the Fiesta crunching against the brittle ice and snow as he backs out into the street. And I can hear the old car for a few fading blocks before the sound dies out altogether.

I stay outside for as long as the cold'll let me and when I go in, Emily is on the couch, laying down, her eyes closed, the living room dark for daylight, the blinds to the backyard drawn and the TV on static. The Christmas tree in the corner has already started to wilt but she plugged the lights in and, lit up, it looks new.

I sit on the edge of the couch with my leg folded under and I run my hand along her shoulder as gently as I can. She smiles and opens her eyes slowly and she looks up at me still with the same pure smile. "Where'd you go?" she asks.

"You didn't see my note?"

"No. I just came down to clean up a little."

"I—we went out. Got some breakfast."

"He's doing good?" she asks.

"Em," I say, "I'm sorry I was—I'm sorry—"

She moves her hand to my back, stops me. "Shouldn't sit like that, babe. Your leg."

"It's okay. It'll be okay."

"You know you don't have to keep hurting yourself. You don't have to keep letting it hurt you."

I say, "Yeah," and I push myself up.

Next to the tree there's a tall garbage bag filled with torn wrapping and all the gifts from yesterday are arranged under and around the tree's low branches. She must have found the Legos because they're on top of one of the piles. I hadn't realized when he handed it to me, but in one corner of the box there's a small white store-bought sticker with a cartoon of a reindeer and a note from a shaky hand: "To Jenny, Love Uncle Mark."

I close my eyes and see stars. "Jenny's still asleep?"

"She is. Why?"

I pick up the Lego box. "Will you help me?"

And together we pull some scraps of used paper from the bag and Emily gets tape from the drawer in the kitchen and we piece the scraps together onto the box, cover the whole thing in rough patterns of torn paper, cover the whole thing except for the tag, and we prop it up against Jenny's other unwrapped presents under the tree. And in the light of the tree—the bright red and gold and white and blue bulbs—and the snow outside and the snow on the TV, it looks like maybe it holds something valuable and new.

## METEORS

We drove through a meteor shower in the dark of the early morning as you tried to catch a flight. You kept pointing them out, *wow*ing each time you'd see one shooting across the sky. I missed them all except the last—a long galactic trail of brilliant fire that arced above the horizon. It only lasted an instant before vanishing and I panicked. I reached down to touch your hand, to make sure you hadn't also disappeared in the atmospheric fuzz that seems to snare all good things that dare try to cross through it.

## SHOTGUN RIDER

You ride shotgun for Wells Fargo and you're feeling pretty important. They named a seat for you up on the stage with your long leather duster and your sawed-off side-by-side. This is serious business. It's just you and the driver and the horses and a wagon of gold out under the stars, of which you can see every last one, here in the vast plain of a new territory. Still California probably, though it doesn't really matter. The whole landscape is just possibility—for trouble, for fame. There's nothing else to distinguish one territory from the next. It's just fort to fort at this point, with the occasional town between, some towns friendlier than others. There was that town a week's ride back where you stepped into the bar only to be told they don't serve guys who guard other people's gold.

Some days it's all you can do not to turn to your left and pull the trigger, ride off with the gold all to yourself. No one but the horses would hear the shot and they'd probably ride off with you. All that's really between that life and this one is the right and wrong question of fire or don't and every time you choose not to shoot, the right grows that much stronger in you, each choice like a new fiber of muscle. The further you are along the ride, the less likely you are to do it absent some grand philosophical shift, some tearing of the muscle.

You've heard about it happening though, the sudden snap. The gunshot, the crack of the reins, shotgun rider hauling off with the loot toward Mexico or some other foreign place where the bank's bounty hunters won't find him. There's a lot of time for thinking out here in the desert and it's an awful big sky and it's hard to think that anything you could do would ever matter at all in comparison to the big things of history—the parting of seas, say, or the explosion of a star. You might even wonder what claim any one man could rightfully stake to owning a wagonfull of a mine's ore. Probably already a rich man, too. Wouldn't miss it.

But there are bigger things than money at stake. You're here to watch for outlaws, especially famous outlaws like Black Bart. Wasn't more than five years ago he got you the first time. Out from the bushes in a black derby hat, his face obscured by an upturned flour sack with holes cut for eyes. It was almost exciting. You saw nothing of his gang other than their rifles poking through the bushes. You were outnumbered then and you gave it up easy, not realizing the rifles were just sticks painted black. He marched you off toward the river all the same, made you and the driver lay with your faces in the dirt, took your leather duster. The humiliation of it all. Made you count to a thousand. Celebrities are never what you want them to be.

Still, there was something intriguing about him that first time, his mystique. There was a softness in his bag-framed eyes, the hand on your back more tender than not. And there was the scrap of paper he'd left on your seat, a poem you still carry, something about how still the night gets and the improbability that in all the frontier, all the universe, two people might for a moment simply be with each other.

And now here he is this night, rising out of a dry creek bed, his two-man gang real now. Three black derbies with guns. When you first see them, there's a half-second in which you wonder who these other guys are. The other times had seemed so intimate, so personal. Could it be they were drawn to this by—what?—something other than gold-greed? Like Black Bart's charm. Or the natural human desire not to be alone on this empty frontier that seems to stretch through the clouds and into space. Or maybe it's some primal need to take one's fate into one's own hands, to reject this life of waiting, like waiting here at the heights of the shotgun seat, waiting for the actions of others to determine the course of your life. There's a pinch in your chest, a contraction.

In the next instant, it's decision time. You press the butt of the gun into the flesh of your shoulder. You've got two barrels, two shells loaded, four pellets a piece that'll be flung in a patter that expands as it flies, quickly loses momentum. They're knock-down shots at best. The kill shots are in the bag of shells at your feet and against three guys you'd almost surely lose the race to reload. Your finger feels for the trigger.

Bart calls out to you. "This isn't the life you wanted," he says.

He sets his gun on the dirt, raises his arms, pulls off the flour sack, and you can see his face now and it's not the outlaw you expected. Older than the pictures you've seen. Long gray mustache and chin beard. Thin tanned face. Wrinkles at the corners of his eyes. He's a man who smiles, you think, who laughs. There's a sweetness to his cracked lips.

He walks toward the coach, each step hitting dirt like a quake. "You want revenge on me, go ahead. But you know it won't do anything to calm your soul. We have so little time left here on this frontier. Wagons're closing in. City's closing in. Is this how you want to live?"

It's quiet then. There's the occasional buck of a horse, but otherwise the scene is still, the scene waits for action to unfold, waits for you to make a choice, the scene itself like a shotgun rider.

Except: You hear the driver behind you reach under the bench seat for his gun. His breath has quickened and you can sense the sweat in his palms, the wild rapids of thought rushing between *shoot* and *run*. He wasn't trained for this.

At this moment, probably you don't think, but if you do, your thought is of the explosion of a star, the new galaxy that's created, the worlds birthed into existence, the mountains formed, the gold buried in them. And the rip feels more like a strain, and you turn to your left and pull and the driver is propelled backward like a sack of flour, upturned, what's left of his face striking dirt first, his eyes suddenly soft and blank, his body limp, lifeless.

Maybe then there's regret, the shot seeming to echo and echo. Or maybe once it's torn it doesn't immediately repair and you swing back the other way and Bart is three steps closer to the gold, this gold now your gold, and you can smell the tobacco in his jacket pocket. There's that sweet smell of tobacco and sweat and the broken smell of gunpowder.

## USED TO BE OCEAN

I said I'd been to a place that used to be the bottom of the ocean but she refused to believe me. "There's no 'used to be' ocean," she said. "Oceans don't disappear. They're too big to change that much." Even after I showed her the brochure, she still wouldn't buy it. I guess somewhere along the line I stopped being believable to her.

"But everything changes," I said. "Everything used to be something else." I regretted then having told her before that aliens built the pyramids and Iceland, with all its geysers and red rock, is actually Mars, and the moon landing was faked, just like the assassination of JFK. They're a defense mechanism, these stories, and also I suppose my way of making things fun when otherwise there'd probably just be the boringness of our empty days. Except now there was nothing I could throw out that'd fold her back in—weather, math problems, compass directions, nothing.

So I drove us there, showed her the signs on the highway. At the guard shack, she asked for evidence we wouldn't drown, that we wouldn't be crushed under the skyscraping weight of water.

"Babe," I said, "they made it into a national park."

Out in the alien landscape, among the gray boulders and the tall gray sea walls, she stopped and leaned back against the car and shook her head. She had red hair that day and her skin was pale white and she made that little twist with her nose. There was wind and her skirt floated up and she pressed it back down to her thighs. Her face flushed. And I remember thinking she looked like she belonged there at the bottom of the sea. Not that she looked like a fish, but maybe like a mermaid or a handsome squid.

"It doesn't make any sense," she said. It's a phrase she's been repeating recently and I've learned she always bites her lip before she says it. It's a dead giveaway and while she speaks I'm already thinking of ways to make everything make sense to her. Like she'd believe me if I tried.

Though she let me pull her to the ground and I took her hand and pressed it into the sediment. Felt the limestone with our fingertips, felt the otherness of it, the something else it once was. I think that was the first time in a while I'd seen her smile; still it was different than before, flatter. She'd been keeping her hair longer, too, and there was a period of time when she wouldn't leave the house without me, when she'd stay a step behind, ride alone in the back seat, in the quiet of it.

It was hot there at the old bottom of the ocean, and so we went into the visitors' center and learned about how cold it used to be where we'd been standing. There was a dark showroom with a recorded narrator that told us all about the place, about the waterpocket, the monocline formed by the deep compressive forces of the laramide to produce the hundred-mile fold with old rocks exposed to the west and a steep dip of new baby rocks to the east. She gave it all her attention.

*//////////*

That night we were back at our hotel and she was studying the book she bought in the gift shop. There was a painting over the bed, one of those motel prints of a seashore in pastels and she laid on the bed in a t-shirt and underwear. Pressed together, her legs were long and finlike. Her skin was burnt from the sun and her red hair was spread out against the white pillowcase. There was something not human about her then, like maybe she was in fact a mermaid or something else I didn't know.

And I don't know if I was angry or sad or if I'd just started to think about how much we hadn't said to each other, how much of her now I'd had to rewrite in my mind, to make up. But whatever it was, for whatever reason, that's when I told her that aliens live among us, that they walk around like people, how our whole idea of what it means to be alive is based on this lie, on aliens' imitation of what humans are supposed to do. I told her aliens need saltwater to survive, that they were the ones who drank our desert ocean dry. And she smiled that flat smile and she closed her eyes and I could tell some part of her was trying hard to believe.

# RESOLUTION

This is the music that plays when he's running to the train station to catch her before she leaves for good, when he finally knows the stakes, he's been pushed into a corner and he's had to make a choice. A strong lead, a sense of fighting against the current, the tide coming in, the melody pushing him back, representing sameness, status quo. But the lead fights against it, a stringy guitar battling minor chords. Maybe he's changed, or at least we're meant to assume he has, because nobody runs through streets like that except when they're charged with guilt and passion, when they've changed. Not entirely, of course. No one changes entirely. We are all who we are. History, instinct, experience: You can't just pack 'em in a suitcase and send 'em off to sea. "Like Yasser fuckin' Arafat, never a night in the same place." But he's pivoted. Backed out of that dead-end corner of the maze and pressed out into the twists and turns, the roundabouts, fighting renewed and stronger, like a train riding frictionless between the rails. He's slipped what chases him and made a turn, become a better version of himself. Gone from passive to active, running hard at the walls.

It's never New York City; New York City's too dirty. But if it were, there would be long shots of the water towers at the heights of the buildings on the Lower East Side and she'd be at Grand Central, the floors would be pristine (none of the usual black stains from gum and grime and footprints) and it would be rush hour and all the men in the terminal would be wearing wide brimmed hats. But it's not New York City. It's somewhere foreign but familiar, an American Belfast or Shanghai. Or it's the Midwest maybe, Chicago or Grand Rapids, the metaphor of fighting the wind or the current.

Of course the train hasn't left yet, though we question the timing. She supposedly left an hour ago. And of course it's raining—it's always raining at this point. Him with his slicked back hair. The lead guitar and the keyboards in disharmony. Car to car, jumping to look in the window, to find her, instead finding fat, floppy old women in peach-colored dresses with feathered hats and boas and large tan suitcases that require their husbands to tip the poor redcap that hauled the things all the way through the station.

Just as all hope seems lost and he's resigned, crushed, he looks up the tracks, toward the front of the train and the tracks stretching into the plains. And she's in line to board in her plasticky red raincoat and clear plastic umbrella, black roller bag and purse, ticket in hand being rained upon. And he shouts to her: "Emily!" or "Emma!" or "Evelyn!" or "Evaline!" Something with an "E" and cute, like her. But she can't hear him, what with the people and the thunder and the steam rising from the cold rain meeting the hot engine sounding a hiss or maybe she has her iPod on or maybe she doesn't want to talk to him (maybe she's passed that point where she says, "Son of a gun, maybe that could'a been something, but the spell's been snapped, I'm no longer feeling it"). He has to get to her, physically, grab her by the shoulders, spin her around, and kiss her. And by that simple act she'll know he's real and he's sorry.

He pushes through the crowd, past tall 1950s-looking men in their long khaki coats, talking on cell phones in the rain. The orchestral anti-harmony underpins the lead, pressing up against it, two separate songs colliding. Here's the crescendo, the rising, the stringy guitar and the chords coming together, meeting on an unexpected note, joining harmonies. And at the last part of the last chance moment comes the resolution. He reaches her, reaches out to her, grabs the shoulders, does the spin thing, says whatever it was he should have said but didn't. "I love you" or "I was wrong" or "I'm sorry" or something like that—one of those things we don't say near often enough or near as often as we should, much as we may mean it and want to say it. It's never as easy as we're meant to believe. All the story lines, all the musical strains, have come together now, and the whole thing wraps itself into a delightful package, into a melody that we've sensed all along. And she steps down from the train and they kiss and cue the end titles.

## OUTLINE OF THE MOON

The first astronauts were launched by a giant slingshot looped around two buildings and pulled taut by a team of oxen. They launched on the day of the Earth's fastest rotation, the Tornos, and the government erected a tall hourglass at the center of the city. A crowd gathered to watch and they counted down, the anticipation building with each of the last few grains until the sling released and the two-man crew shot up through flocks of birds and through storm clouds, into the purple layers beyond. The pilot cranked the ship's wings while the navigator kept them on course as they flew further out through the air's outer shell and at last they slipped into the black of space. It was very dark.

They'd commissioned the ship specifically for this flight, found the best cooper they could to build a barrel big enough to fit the crew and all of their scientific equipment. The front end was a cone and they'd painted the outside with the flags of the great explorers—Magellan and de Gama and Marco Polo and Cortez. When it was finished, the men stood back, admired the craft against the crescent moon. They named their ship the *Jules Verne*.

It's always nighttime in space. The pilot had stowed a blanket in the wooden cabin in case either man got cold, and he and the navigator huddled together underneath it, pulled it over their heads. The navigator had a flashlight and a book of fairy tales and he and the pilot took turns reading aloud. The lids of their eyes seemed to weigh less in space, but they were both exhausted from their months of training and from the force of the launch. Before they slept, the pilot set an alarm; he knew the navigator could sometimes get too involved in a dream and accidentally sleep late but their time was short and they had work to do.

///////////////

They woke to the moon rising in the window, not as a shifting shape or a blinking eye like they expected from its always-changing arc in their home sky. Nor was it the flat disc some of their friends had guessed. It was a big round ball: plain, dusty, and, though neither would say it, disappointing somehow.

The navigator brewed coffee and squeezed juice from the sack of oranges they'd brought on board, and the pilot cooked bacon and eggs. The smell reminded them both of Sunday mornings, of home. After breakfast, they pressed tracing paper against the window of the *Verne* and the navigator took a pencil around the outline of the moon and shaded also the dark depressions on its surface, places where, they imagined, others had come and rudely scooped out souvenirs. Their mission wasn't to return a piece of the moon but just to touch it, to confirm that it's real. Sometimes it seemed like the world was all water, all wave, that they might drown in the rising, receding, and disappearing of things. But the moon was always there.

There was a dangerous time, then, as they got closer, and the pilot slowed the *Verne* and the navigator twisted and turned it, tried to find the right angle of approach. They'd practiced the landing at home on the beach in Carolina, laughed at the small-thinking Wrights up the way.

And now here at the moon. The pilot and the navigator landed the craft. Soft and safe. The *Verne*'s wooden feet made shallow moon dimples.

They both took deep breaths to hold and opened the door. The navigator went first. He stepped out onto the surface, which glowed through the dust at his feet. The pilot knelt, set his hand on the moon, felt it on the pads of his fingers, thought for a moment that he was at the bottom of it, like he was holding it in his palm, holding it up.

The navigator watched the stars; they seemed more alive here, like they'd brightened and grown in the long night it had taken the Verne to get here. One star burst like a firework.

*/////////////*

Once they got tired of exploring, the pilot climbed back into the ship and the navigator gave it a strong push before jumping in and closing the door. The pilot flapped the wings while the navigator turned the handle on the rake they'd hooked onto one of the legs of the Verne and combed over the marks they'd left on the surface, made the moon new again, like they'd never been there.

Without the moon in the window, night lasted longer, and with the excitement of the new moon passed, they seemed to fly slower. It felt colder, too, and they stayed under the blanket for most of the trip. This time they took turns telling scary stories and neither could sleep. They hadn't realized before how high up they were, how far from home they were, how blank the black sky was without even a cloud to spark their imaginations.

They had to be getting close, the pilot said. He'd been counting the hours in his head and his idea of time was always pretty good. But it was nighttime at home and the world was dark and it blended into space so that they couldn't see it. And there was a moment when they both feared that maybe it was gone, that they were alone up here. Or that maybe they'd been alone all along, that maybe Earth was the dream and home was just something they'd both imagined. Maybe they were space creatures, aliens lost without a planet, flying this one long aimless night in the Verne, the walls of the wooden ship rattled by the pull of passing stars.

And that's when they saw it: the flash of a lighthouse and another flash and then more flashes as the beam circled. They went toward it, sank into the atmosphere. The navigator pulled a lever releasing a balloon from the nose of the Verne and he struck a match. The balloon filled with hot air and lofted them down to Earth, to the lighthouse, back to shore.

////////////

Years later, after the parades and ceremonies, the radio show appearances, the keys to cities and the honorary degrees, the pilot and the navigator met at a dock near the ocean. Each carried a coffee can and his uniform and boots, the boots unworn since splashdown, each uniform neatly pressed and folded and showing the sewn-on insignia of the *Verne*, just as the museum had requested.

They sat at the edge of the dock and watched the waves. Even after so long, there was nothing new either could think to say. The journey and the moon were just memories now, locked away in the same small place every other day went, no sharper or louder than another day's lunch or the words of a book they'd read long ago. Neither wanted to look up. There was something, maybe, about the mysteries of things being less, about how far away space could be so much more knowable than the water at their feet.

After a while, the navigator reached for the coffee cans and the pilot reached for the boots. One by one, the pilot turned the boots on end and emptied the dust, shook each of his boots over one can and each of the navigator's boots over the other. When they were done, the pilot closed the lids and set the cans between them. And the pilot and the navigator looked back to the water, the dark sea, and watched for the lights of ships coming into harbor.

# ACKNOWLEDGMENTS

So here we are at the end, a point that would never have been reached, that would never have existed, without the love and everything of a great number of people, from whom I've learned more than I'll ever be able to repay and of whom I'll name just a few here: Caitlin; Sallie and Roger (Mom and Dad); Midge and Dan; Ben, Maddie, and Nate; Nora; Deo; Marcos L. Martínez, Justin Lafreniere, and the brilliant Stillhouse team; Dan Pickard; David Bajo, Elise Blackwell, Ed Madden, and Alexander Ogden; the weirdo writers, Lauren Eyler and Justin Brouckaert; my co-editors Brandon Rushton and Jennifer Blevins; Andrew, MC, William, Chris, Rebecca, and my SCMFA cohort; the Squaw Valley Community of Writers, the Wesleyan Writers Workshop, the New Harmony Writers Workshop; the "Sevens": Kelly Luce, Andrew Dugas, Krista Minard, Caitlin Myer, Nora Boxer, Matt Monte, Kristin FitzPatrick, A.R. Taylor, Eric Aragon, Lois Rosen, Mike Shaler, Shanda Connolly; Paul Rudd; Grace and Joy; Kimberly Elkins, Alex Espinoza, Jackie Livesay, Bill Johnson, Karen Lamott; Ethan Miller, Derek Hills, Kate Schuler, Stephanie Svec; Joe Donnelly, Murphy McHugh, Erik Harrison; Ian MacFarland, Bob Apel, and all the kids from the neighborhood; Candis Mitchell, Nicky and Martijn Veltman; Rory Diamond; Tim Johnston, Mike Czyzniejewski, Justin Daugherty, Matt Sailor, Christian Kiefer; Barbara Morgan and Christa McAuliffe; the crew at *Passages North*; Annie Dillard, Stuart Dybek, George Saunders, Etgar Keret, and John Hughes. And there are many many more family, friends, and strangers who've contributed in one way or another to this book. I'm indescribably grateful to you all.

Thanks also to the editors of the publications in which these stories first appeared (sometimes in slightly different form): "The Pilot" in *alice blue review*; "Open Mic and Drafts on Special and All the Players are Local and Bad" in *Atticus Review*; "River to Shanghai" in *Belleville Park Pages*; "Bigfoot's Overcoat" in *Cosmonaut's Avenue*; "Kill TV" in *Day One*; "Legend of Link and Z" in *Everyday Genius*; "Air Raid," "Hangman" (as "Stealing Copper"), and "Willow" in *FRiGG Magazine*; "Tonto Rides a Bus to Visit His Mother-in-Law, Who is Dying From Cancer" in *jmww*; "Used to Be Ocean" in *Juked*; "What Exists in this Dojo" in *Karate Kid 30th Anniversary Anthology*; "Meteors" and "We are Swimmers" in *Moon City Review*; "The Rust Belt" in *NANO Fiction*; "In the Shape of" in *New Flash Fiction Review*; "Old Plymouth" in *New South*; "Shotgun Rider" in *PANK*; "Frozen Alive" (as "Frozen") in *Paper Nautilus*; "Extinction Event," "Outline of the Moon," and "Maybe Mermaids and Robots are Lonely" in *Passages North*; "A Monster for Always" in *Pinball*; "Fireworks" in *Pithead Chapel* and in *Vestal Review* (winner of the 2014 Flash Fiction Award); "Finishing Moves [when it comes crashing down]" in *Quiddity*; "The Allegory of the Boxer and the Spy" (as "The Boxer and the Spy") in *Revolution John*; "Pearls" in *RPM: Fiction with Torque Anthology* (Split Lip Press) and (as "Salt Atlas") in *A Sense of the Midlands Anthology* (Muddy Ford Press); "White Smoke" in *Smokelong Quarterly*; "Beach Glass" in *Squalorly*; "Plain Burial" in *Story|Houston*; "Cardboard Graceland" in *Sundog Lit*; and "Resolution" (as "Denouement") in *Zero Ducats* (also adapted as a short film as part of the Expecting Goodness Film Festival).

.

This book would not have been possible without
the hard work of our staff.

We would like to acknowledge:

***Justin Lafreniere, Managing Editor***

Marcos L. Martínez, Editor-in-Chief
Meghan McNamara, Director of Media & Communications
Douglas J. Luman, Art Director
Alex Walsh, Cover Art Designer
Scott W. Berg, Editorial Advisor

**stillhouse
press**

ASSISTANT EDITORS

Madeline Dell'Aria
Kyle Freelander

EDITORIAL INTERNS

Kelly Foster
Abigail Casas
Ben Rader
Suzy Rigdon
Hailey Scherer
Qinglan Wang

OUR DONORS

Maziar Gahvari
Gerald Prout

Matthew Fogarty's work has appeared in *Passages North, Fourteen Hills, PANK, The Rumpus, Midwestern Gothic*, and elsewhere. He has twice been a finalist for the Write-a-House residency, and has received scholarships from the New Harmony Writers Workshop, the Wesleyan Writers Conference, and the Squaw Valley Community of Writers. He earned his MFA at the University of South Carolina, where he served as the Editor of *Yemassee*. Currently, Fogarty is a Co-Publisher of Jellyfish Highway. He is originally from Troy, Michigan, one of the square-mile suburbs of Detroit.

CPSIA information can be obtained
at www.ICGtesting.com
Printed in the USA
BVHW04s0624220518
516996BV00001B/4/P

9 780990 516941